EMPRESS OF THE GALAXY

BOOK TWO

USA TODAY BESTSELLING AUTHOR
CATHERINE BANKS

EMPRESS OF THE GALAXY

⊰━━◯━━⊱ 2 ⊰━━◯━━⊱

THEIR FAE GODDESS

Empress of the Galaxy by Catherine Banks.

Copyright © 2019 Catherine Banks

Cover design by Ana Cruz Arts.

Published by Turbo Kitten Industries.

www.CatherineBanks.com

Turbo Kitten Industries™, P.O. Box 5012, Galt, CA 95632

Acknowledgments

Thank you to the following people who helped make this book possible:

C.R. for being such a fantastic person and helping me in ways she may never realize.

Lea for being awesome and helping me in so many ways.

Jenica for always being there. She means more to me than she knows.

As always, my amazing husband and best friend, Avery.

Thank you also to my amazing Kickstarter supporters:
Alicia Rades
Andromeda Taylor-Wallace
Annette McElroy
Betheny Thompson
Brooke
Candace Wondrak
Christina
Christina Hunt
Claire Ellison
Daniel Tice Jr
Derek Murphy
Helen Scott
Jacqueline Hayley
Jathan McBride
Kaiya Kagon

Jennifer Laslie

Jessica Paige

Jessica Robbins

Karri Allen

Altheda Rutherford

Kathy

Kristal Melton

Lance McKee

Leslie Twitchell

Marie Andreas

Mettie A.M.

Winter Bruno

Michael Green

Michelle McFarlin

Nikki Jefford

Sunny Side Up

Cali Mann

Rachel Strehlow

Shannon

Sky A Fallows

Stephanie Meier

Stuart March

Tanya

Wanda

Jaycee DeLorenzo

CHAPTER I
ELARA

"I NEED an audience with the Unseelie Court. I need to see the Unseelie King, or whoever their ruler is, specifically."

The five men in front of me wore varying shades of disbelief. The Four Warlords of Minloa were my guards and soon to be my mates. The fifth man was my guard and soon to be mate as well, Ryul. He'd been my friend when we were children, and had waited a thousand years for me to return to him.

"Absolutely not," Kydrus growled, his sharp canines showing.

"No," Ryul snapped.

"Why?" Durlan asked.

"There are some wrongs that need righted," I said and then grimaced. "I actually have a lot of travel I need to make."

"You're talking crazy," Amrynn said. "Where is this all coming from?"

Venali was the only one who hadn't spoken. Instead, he chose to glower at me, his eyes sparkling with an emotion I couldn't quite place.

"Have any of you been to Eltare before?" I asked.

The Unseelie had been forced out of Minloa, and lived on an island near our continent. I wasn't sure how many Unseelie there were, but it had to be rather crowded for them to all fit on the island.

"No, none of us have been there," Venali answered when everyone else chose to stare at me silently. "And, I don't think it's wise for you to go there either."

"I guess we'll just have to travel the old-fashioned way," I said, ignoring his second comment. "By boat."

"You keep ignoring our questions," Ryul growled.

I sighed and ran a hand down my face. "It's complicated. I don't really want to get into it right now. The best thing we can do is sleep and then discuss our travel plans tomorrow."

"You said you have a lot of travel. Where else are you wanting to go?" Durlan asked.

He was the only one who seemed calm, though his frown led me to believe he didn't want me to go, like the other four.

I rubbed the back of my neck, turned away from them, and grimaced at the pain in my head.

"What's wrong?" Amrynn asked, coming to my side.

Of course he would know I was in pain without facing him. Our time alone had connected us a bit more than I liked to admit. And this new connection...I wasn't sure what to think about it yet. I knew what it was, but I wanted to stay in my land of denial, so I wouldn't even think of the name.

"Headache," I whispered, but that wasn't completely true. My head did hurt, but it was from holding back my power. I didn't want to be a goddess. I didn't want to be Amara. I was Elara, dammit.

I swayed on my feet, and Amrynn wrapped an arm

around me to keep me upright.

"You're burning up," he growled, picked me up in his arms and carried me to my room. "What's wrong, Elara? Why are you ill?"

"She's being stubborn," Ryul growled. "Stop denying it and open yourself to the power. I can see it boiling within you."

Curse him and his stupid sight.

"What?" Venali asked him.

Ryul placed his hand on my forehead and stared into my eyes. "Elara, just admit it to yourself and let the power out."

"No," I growled. "I am Elara, heir to Minloa. That is all."

"You are Amara, Goddess and ruler of the universe," he corrected.

I growled at him. "Don't say that name. I already ordered you to not say that name."

He scowled at me. "Really?"

"Get out," I ordered him.

His hand dropped to his side. "What?"

"Get out of my room, Ryul," I snapped.

Venali set a hand on his shoulder. "Come talk to me outside." In a quieter voice, one he probably thought I couldn't hear, he said, "I need you to tell us more about what you know."

Ryul's eyes flashed, pain and anger both in his expression, but he finally lowered his gaze in submission and left.

All of my guards left, shutting my door as they did.

I relaxed on my bed and closed my eyes. I wasn't going to let her win. I wasn't her. I was Elara. I was Elara.

Elara.

Elara.

CHAPTER 2

AMRYNN

"SHE'S REFUSING to accept who she really is," Ryul said, glaring at the door as though he could still see Elara. "If she doesn't accept it, the power will make her more ill, and it could kill her."

"Why doesn't she want to admit it?" I asked.

My future mate was a stubborn and prideful woman, but I couldn't believe she would do something that could ultimately kill her. She was a goddess, reincarnated. Why wouldn't she want to admit that?

"I don't know. I wasn't alive the last time Amara was here, but we bear her marks on us. We are her consorts," Ryul answered. He ran a hand through his hair and exhaled loudly. "She kicked me out. I can't believe she kicked me out."

"You did say the name again, after she ordered us not to," Kydrus reminded him.

Ryul glared at him. "She has to accept it."

"Forcing her will do nothing but cause her to shut down

more. She is stubborn and hates being ordered to do anything," Venali said. "She has to make the decision on her own."

"What if she doesn't?" Durlan asked, lifting his head to look at us. "What if she refuses to accept it and gets worse?"

None of us had an answer for that.

The thought of losing her made my heart twist and my gut drop. I'd almost lost her to Barry. I had been useless then, and I was useless now. I hated it. Oh, how I hated it.

"We should just give her the space she wants tonight," I said and swallowed the fear down.

"What are we going to do about her wanting to go to the Unseelie?" Durlan asked.

"We cannot let her go," Venali growled.

"She's going to go," I mumbled. "Whether we help her or not."

"She can't teleport on this planet. So, we should be fine," Kydrus said.

I scoffed. "She'll sneak out the first chance she gets. If she wants to go, she will. So, you all need to determine if you are willing to go with her or not."

"You're willing to let her go and face them? Those barbarians?" Kydrus asked, his eyes narrowed.

"I would rather she never leave Durlan's house again, but it is not up to me. She will go, and I will guard her. That is my job. Wherever she goes, I go," I answered.

Durlan sighed. "I'm afraid he's right. She will go, despite our opinions."

Venali growled and stalked out of the house and into the night. Knowing him, he was probably going to punch something until he destroyed it.

"I'll do some research," Durlan said, turning towards his study. "Everyone, just keep an eye on her, but don't go in her room or engage her."

"This is ridiculous," Ryul growled.

"We all agree," I said. "But there is little we can do."

CHAPTER 3
VENALI

ELARA WAS FINALLY MINE. My mate. Yet, now more issues had arisen.

Amara.

Had I not been marked as well, I might not have believed it. She was our goddess. A fable, myth, that we told the children. How was it possible that Elara was her?

And, if I was her consort, did that mean I was a reincarnation of one of Amara's consorts, too?

I punched a tree, a hole forming in the wake of my fist.

If Elara didn't accept her power, she would die. I couldn't let her die. I'd thought she was lost before. I refused to watch her wither away now.

But she wanted to see the Unseelie. That also made no sense.

The Unseelie would steal her away or kill her, if given the chance.

I didn't want to take her to them, but if I didn't go, she would leave me behind and I would always wonder if I could have saved her.

This felt like a suicide mission. But, if I could save her, I would gladly forfeit my life.

No, we would all survive this. They would not kill us.

I would kill every last Unseelie if they hurt her. Or die trying.

CHAPTER 4
KYDRUS

MY MIND WAS STILL REELING from our revelations. Elara wanted me as a mate. She had accepted me, and then a symbol, one not seen for over two thousand years appeared on all of us.

Not only was she queen, but she was also the missing goddess.

Amrynn, Ryul, Durlan, and Venali sat around Durlan's study, all deep in their own thoughts. All were as worried as I was that our mate wanted to go speak to the ruler of the Unseelie.

Another thought occurred to me.

"Didn't Amara have seven consorts?" I voiced my thought.

Venali let loose a string of curses.

"Yes," Durlan answered. "I was thinking about that, too."

"Are you telling me two more guys are going to show up with the symbols on their necks?" Ryul asked, his jaw clenched and the words barely slipping out. His hands glowed and would likely become coated in flames if he didn't control his anger.

"Yes," Durlan said with a frown.

The blue flames erupted over Ryul's hands and up his forearms.

Venali growled loudly.

I tossed Venali a long log from beside the fireplace, which he promptly snapped in half.

I should have felt the same, but I was rather accepting for some reason.

"Who else could rival us in power?" Amrynn asked. "Not to brag, but I haven't run across anyone in Minloa who was nearly as powerful as us."

"She did mention that she has a lot of traveling to do. Maybe that's why. Maybe she needs to travel to another continent to find her last mates," Durlan said. His normally relaxed expression hardened. "I hate sailing."

Laughter burst out of me, uncontrollable and loud.

Durlan arched a brow.

"You're not worried about our mate finding more mates, ones we don't know. No, you're worried about sailing," I gasped.

He sighed. "I have accepted my fate. I am her guard and mate, I already share her with you four, so what's two more?"

"I don't like this," Ryul growled.

"It is what it is," I said and sat back, looking up at the ceiling. "Who knew such a timid creature would cause so much trouble in my life."

Venali leaned forward. "How are we going to travel to another continent? We can't leave our sectors unwatched for more than a week."

"I don't know," Durlan admitted. "I'm still trying to figure that out."

We lapsed back into silence, none of us coming up with an answer. We didn't want to leave our sectors, but Elara leaving without us was even more unacceptable. I'd been separated from her once, with no knowledge of whether she was alive or not. I would not do the same now. I would go insane wondering if she was alright, and if she did get injured, I would blame myself for not being there to protect her.

"Perhaps it is time we found new warlords," Amrynn said. "We could announce Elara, hold a tournament, and then we could all go with her."

I sighed but agreed. "I second this idea."

"You've changed," Venali said, lifting a brow. "Old Kydrus would have torn into Amrynn for suggesting such a thing."

"Old Kydrus wasn't a consort to a goddess, or mate to a queen. I have different priorities now. I won't stay here while she travels for months."

He growled and lowered his head, glaring at his hands. "Announcing her as queen and then disappearing for several months isn't exactly a great plan."

"She will be going on a diplomatic expedition," Durian said. "Royals used to do it all the time."

"Not immediately after taking the throne," Venali countered.

"Then we make her wait a month," I said.

Ryul rubbed at his chest, grimacing. "If she survives that long."

He had different magic than us, which apparently let him

see her power. If he was right, we had to convince her to accept who she truly was as soon as possible.

"One thing at a time," Durlan said. "Amrynn, go tell Elara our plan."

"Why him?" Venali bristled.

"Because he can control his emotions and he spent the most time with her." Durlan sighed and rubbed the back of his neck, shoulders slumped.

Technically, I had spent the most time with her, but now was not the time to argue that point.

Amrynn stood and nodded. "I'll come back and let you know how it went."

CHAPTER 5
ELARA

My body burned and sweat poured down my face. I wanted to scream or punch someone. Maybe both.

"I am Elara, heir to Minloa," I growled for the thirtieth time since my mates had left me alone in my room. "I will not give in."

Maybe if I used just a bit of the magic, it would ease my suffering.

With a deep breath, I drew a tiny amount of my power out. It tried to escape in a tornado, but I held it at bay. The power came to me, and I used it to reach down the new bond with my mates. There should have only been five, but two additional bonds, not fully completed, glowed as well.

The two bonds tugged, trying to find me, to communicate. I slammed my barriers shut, using the power to wall myself off.

No. Not now. Now was not the time. Not yet.

Someone knocked on my door, so I quickly sealed my power again, bottling it up tight.

Surprisingly, I did feel better. I wiped my face and sat up.

"Come in," I called.

Amrynn entered, a scowl of worry marring his handsome face. When he saw me sitting up, the scowl lessened. "How are you feeling?"

"Better," I answered truthfully.

He sat on the end of my bed, examining me. "We've decided on a course of action."

I glared. "Without me present."

He smiled. "Easy, Elara."

I sighed. "Go on."

"We're going to announce you. We are also going to hold a tournament to replace ourselves as warlords."

My mouth dropped open. "What? I don't understand. You all agreed to be my mates. We're bound magically, for eternity. And *now* you want to back out?" I stood, facing him with tears in my eyes. "I know you guys are upset that I haven't accepted this...development, but—"

He stood and gripped my upper arms, tightly, but not enough to hurt. "Elara, let me finish. We aren't backing out. We are your mates, now and forever."

Tears dripped down my cheek, and I sniffed loudly. "Okay."

He stroked his hands up and down my arms, while smiling softly. "We don't want to separate from you, especially not when you're going into enemy territory. However, we can't leave our sectors unattended either."

Okay, that made sense. My tears subsided, and I sniffed again, my fear and heartbreak gone.

"So, we're going to hold a tournament to find new warlords. That way we can leave Minloa in their hands," he continued.

"That's great," I said. "I'm totally on board with this."

He sat back on the bed, crossing one leg over the other. My eyes were drawn to his mouth as he resumed speaking. "After the tournament, you need to be here for at least a month, though."

"What? Why?" I asked, jerking my gaze up to his eyes.

"The new queen can't just disappear for months right after taking up the mantle. You need to get things in motion and in order first," he explained.

I sighed and dropped my head forward. "You're just trying to keep me from going to the Unseelie."

"No. We all know you are going to go, and nothing we do will keep you from that. We are really just trying to get things set up correctly."

I looked up at him, scowling. "I need to see the Unseelie."

He scowled. "Is one of your other consorts Unseelie?"

My eyes widened and my mouth popped open. "You know about the others?"

He smirked. "She-who-shall-not-be-named had seven consorts. We assumed you would as well."

Crap.

"Is one of them Unseelie?" he asked.

"I don't know," I answered. "I can sense them, but I've blocked the bonds so they can't find me or contact me."

"Why?" he asked, titling his head slightly to the side.

I fidgeted with my shirt. "I'm not ready yet. We just confirmed our bonds. I don't want to add two more into the mix. I know it's going to be difficult for you guys to deal with."

"Only a couple of us are upset about it, but they'll come around," he assured me.

I sat on his lap and rested my head on his shoulder. "I don't want this," I whispered. "I just wanted us to become mates, and for me to take the throne with you five at my side."

Amrynn wrapped his arms around me, holding me tightly. "We are here for you. Always will be. We will get through this together. But you have to be honest with us. You have to trust us and give us as much information as you can."

"There are some things that are best left to discuss later," I mumbled, turning my face into his shirt. "Other things, I don't want to know."

"You're still feverish," he whispered. "Why won't you accept it? What is it that frightens you?"

"I don't want to be a celestial. I went from being a slave to being a Seelie queen. Isn't that enough of a jump for one lifetime?"

"You promise you won't let this kill you?" he whispered.

I nodded. "I'm not that stubborn."

He chuckled, but it was tense.

"When are you going to announce me?" I asked him, stroking my fingertips along his throat. I wanted to touch more of his skin, but since he was dressed, this was the best I could do at the moment.

"Tomorrow."

I tensed. Everything was going to change in the next few months. I wasn't sure if I was ready.

And my poor mates. They were going to give up their titles for me. It wasn't fair.

"Maybe you—"

"We are voluntarily giving up our titles as warlords," Amrynn said, interrupting me. "We are not being forced. We want to be with you much more than we want to stay warlords."

How did he know I was going to say that?

"Will you lie with me for a bit?" I asked and chewed on my lip nervously.

Without hesitation, he pulled off his boots, laid us down, and pulled a blanket up over us both. He spooned his body around mine and kissed the side of my neck. "Rest, my queen. I will keep you safe."

CHAPTER 6
RYUL

"She's sleeping now," Amrynn informed us as he stepped out of her bedroom. He shut her door and motioned at us to follow him to the living room.

"How did she take the news?" I asked.

"Surprisingly well," he said as he sat. "And, she admitted she does have two other mates, but she's blocked their bonds so they can't find her or communicate with her."

All of us grimaced.

I didn't want her to have more mates, but to have your mate block you and refuse to communicate with you would be torturous.

"Does she know who they are?" I asked. Not that it mattered. I had no say in any of this.

Amrynn shook his head and sighed. "She's overwhelmed. She had no idea this was going to happen, and wants to enjoy having us as mates first."

"Overwhelmed?" Kydrus asked. "I'm not surprised."

"She did go from being a slave to all of this rather quickly," Durlan said. "It's a huge change."

"So, she's fine with waiting for the tournament and a month after to go to the Unseelie?" Venali asked, folding his arms over his chest.

Amrynn nodded. "She understands our reasoning and said she is fine with it. She..." He looked down at his hands and sighed loudly. "When I told her we were finding new warlords, she thought we were abandoning her."

"What?" My anger skyrocketed, heat rushing to my face. After all we had been through? Could any of us even consider abandoning her?

"How could she think that?" Venali asked, his voice more growl than usual. "We're bound for eternity."

Amrynn looked up at me, and then Venali. "She's terrified of being abandoned. I can't say I blame her. Before she had her memories, she must have assumed her parents abandoned her to be a slave. She never fit in, and we've been pushing her to learn as much as possible. She needs reassuring. She's young."

"If she would accept her powers, she would regain her previous lives' memories. She would know that we won't ever abandon her," I snapped.

"Ryul, we understand your frustration, but snapping at her or being mad at her won't change anything. It will only make matters worse." Kydrus sighed.

I stood and glared at him. "She let out some of her powers. I felt it. She knows, yet she refuses to fully accept it. It's going to continue to weaken her and can kill her."

"She assured me she won't let it kill her," Amrynn said.

I scoffed. "She's more stubborn than any of you realize. You understand that our memories won't unlock until she accepts her powers as well, right? We'd have a lot more information at our disposal, and I am certain that is part of why she's holding back. She doesn't want us to remember. She doesn't want us to know the secrets she is keeping from us."

I turned and stormed out of the living room and out of the house. They were blinded by their love for her. Blinded by her childlike innocence. I loved her more than anything in all of the worlds, but my magic allowed me to see more than them. She was keeping secrets from us. Secrets I was certain were dangerous.

It bothered me most of all that she wouldn't confide in me. We were friends, weren't we? Why wasn't she confiding in me then? It hurt, but I would never admit that for fear of the others viewing me as weak.

"Want to spar?" Venali asked from behind me.

I stopped walking and turned to face him. "What?"

He smirked. "You look like you could use an outlet for some of that anger. I know I could."

I blew out a breath and nodded. Sparring would help me rein in my anger a bit. Hopefully enough to keep from blowing up at her. I knew Kydrus was right about my anger only making things worse, but it hurt to feel her dying.

"Let me know if her condition becomes serious," Venali said as we headed towards the fighting ring. "If she lets herself deteriorate too much, tell me."

"You think you can do something to change her mind?" I asked, jealousy rearing its head at the thought that he might be closer to her than I was. Part of that was my own fault. I should spend more time with her.

"I'm the brute of this group. She knows this. So, when I come to her and beg her for something, prostrating myself before her, she usually listens. I'm not going to do that until it's absolutely necessary, though," he said with a frown that stretched the scar on his face.

"She needs to wake up," I grumbled.

"You're being too hard on her. She's not as old as us, remember? She's still only in her twenties. Think about what you were like then. We were all naïve and stupid. She's scared and the only way to get her to open up to us is by showing her that she doesn't need to be scared. That we have her back no matter what."

For a brute, he was rather smart.

I sighed and rubbed a hand down my face. "You're right, but I'll stab you if you tell anyone I admitted that."

He laughed and clapped me on the shoulder. "Let's spar. I think there are a few tricks I can teach you that will improve your fighting. If we really are going to the Unseelie, we're going to need to be in the best shape possible."

CHAPTER 7
ELARA

THE ANNOUNCEMENT PROCEDURE was surprisingly simple. The warlords just gathered as many people as they could in their cities, and then spread the word by written decrees. These decrees also announced the tournament, which would happen in just under a week.

"You're sure that you want to give up your titles?" I asked for the fiftieth time.

All four of my warlord mates looked at me with the same expression. Blankness.

They had been reverting to courtly faces a lot around me lately, and it drove me insane.

"Fine, I get it," I grumbled. "You're going to give up your titles so you can travel with me because I'm more important than titles."

Amrynn's lip twitched, the only indication that they heard me.

"Venali, can you come with me?" I asked and stood.

Venali stood without question.

"We'll be back," I said, biting my lip as I headed out of the house.

Venali shut the door behind us, and walked at my side. His towering presence was reassuring.

I moved closer to him, and he threaded our fingers together. Relief surged through me, and I let out a sigh. Of them all, he would be the quietest, let me work things out in my head instead of discussing them, and would know what it was like to need some space.

"Just needed some air?" he asked, rubbing his thumb over the back of my hand.

I nodded.

"You should let me teach you some more fighting moves," he said softly. "So, you are fully prepared for our upcoming travel."

"I agree," I said with a nod. "Tomorrow we can start training."

He smiled down at me, and my heart tightened.

Mine. He was all mine.

I sat on the edge of the hill that overlooked the city below, and he sat behind me, sliding his legs along the outside of mine, and trapped me. I leaned back against his chest and closed my eyes. He wrapped his arms around my body and held me close.

"I love you," he whispered in my ear. "I will always love you. No matter what happens, I will always be by your side. You know that, right?"

I raised my hand and rested it against his cheek, and then turned in his embrace so I could look up into his eyes. "I do, but the reassurance is good."

He kissed my palm, and my heart sped. "You are the

greatest gift I've ever been given. I didn't realize how much I was missing until I found you. You are beautiful, kind, and more stubborn than me."

I chuckled, and snuggled against him, resting my head on his shoulder. "I love you, Venali. I'm sorry for being stubborn."

"You wouldn't be you if you weren't stubborn," he said quietly, and I didn't need to look at him to know he was smiling.

"Can we sit here for a bit?" I snuggled in deeper.

"We can sit here as long as you like." His heartbeat quickened under my heads on his chest.

As long as I liked, ended up being a few hours, and then my stomach reminded me that it was past time to eat.

When we returned, I sat at the table with all of my mates around me, and smiled as we finished eating. As much as I hated that they were giving things up because of me, I preferred having them by my side constantly.

My smile wilted as one of my unclaimed mates tapped at the shield I had put up between us.

He tapped harder, and then slammed against it.

I cried out and doubled over, clutching at my head.

"Elara?" Ryul asked, grimacing as he squatted down beside me.

I reinforced the shield, and straightened. "I'm okay. Sorry."

"As much as I hate to say it, you really should let them in," he whispered.

I took a deep breath and said, "Not yet. It's not time yet."

"How do you know when it will be time?" he asked.

Ryul had been exceptionally snarky before, but he looked curious now, with no anger present.

"I just will," I said. I stood, had to put a hand on the back of my chair to keep my balance, and excused myself to my room.

CHAPTER 8
VENALI

"You're telegraphing your moves," I told Elara. "You don't need to wind up to throw a punch. Anyone who sees you is going to know what you're planning to do."

She sat on the ground, covered in sand and sweat, panting heavily.

I hadn't realized how out of shape she had become. Then again, she could be tired from holding back her powers.

She nodded in understanding and stood up, brushing her palms off. "Okay. How do I stop telegraphing?"

"Throw a punch at me," I ordered her.

She turned her right shoulder, and I held up my hand. "That. You turned your shoulder."

She froze and examined her stance. After a moment, her eyes widened and she whispered, "Oh."

"Let's go inside," I said. "You've done a lot today and learned some."

"I didn't learn much," she muttered, but followed me anyway. She walked with a slight limp, so I picked her up in my arms. She was so light, and soft.

"Hey," she gasped.

"You're limping. I don't want you damaging your muscles. I'll carry you to the shower."

"Will you be joining me?" she asked in a sultry voice and smirked at me.

My cock strained against my pants at the thought of showering with her and touching her naked body. "Yes," I replied immediately.

She relaxed in my arms, and whispered, "We better make it quick. I'm starving."

Inside, we passed by the others, all gathered to go over plans for the tournament. They watched us go, no doubt knowing what we were about to do, but I didn't care.

Inside the bathroom, I set her down on the counter, and then turned the water on to the temperature she preferred, scalding hot. I had no idea how she could stand such hot water, but we were all learning to handle it.

I turned around, and if I hadn't already been aroused, the sight of her naked before me, bruised, sweaty, and sandy would have done me in.

"What?" she asked and looked in the mirror, pushing her hair around. "Is there something on me?"

"Sand," I answered, turning away to undress.

She slid her hands along my back, around my ribs, and hugged me from behind. "I don't know if I can wash my hair. My arms hurt."

I ushered her into the shower. "I'll wash you."

She stepped under the water and sighed. The steam rose around her, and I wondered how long it would be before we could enjoy moments like this again, once she started her journey.

She swiped hair away from her face, and then dropped to her knees and took my erection in her mouth.

I groaned and leaned back against the wall of the shower. Her mouth was warm, wet, and she knew just the right amount of suction to make every logical thought in my head disappear.

I had to resist the urge to grab her head and pump my hips. It would be rude, and she probably wouldn't enjoy it.

Instead, I picked her up, spun her around, and thrust inside her while gripping her hips.

"Yes," she screamed, arching up. Her muscles tightened around me and I groaned loudly.

I was always conflicted. I wanted to finish quickly, but I also wanted to do this all day long and listen her to moans and screams as I made her orgasm again and again.

"Faster," she growled, resting her hand on the wall in front of her.

I obeyed, gripping her hips and thrusting faster and harder. With each orgasm, she grew slicker and slicker, and I grew closer to finishing.

I turned her around, looping one of her legs around my hip, pushed her up against the wall of the shower, claimed her mouth, and then thrust inside of her again.

She gasped into my mouth, which only made me hungrier for her to orgasm again.

She did, moments later, and then I couldn't hold it back anymore, and I finished as well.

I dropped my head to her shoulder, and drew in ragged breaths as my heart returned to a normal beating pattern.

CHAPTER 9
ELARA

THE DAY of the tournament dawned cool and clear. I had expected a large crowd, but it looked like all of Minloa had come.

I stood near the podium where I would be sitting to watch the fights, and surveyed the crowd.

Children ran between people, grabbing snacks from vendors and laughing. People chatted, most with smiles on their faces.

It was strange to see so many people who looked happy. It was even stranger to know they were happy and here to see me.

"Queen Elara," Venali whispered from beside me.

I jumped and reached for my sword, but stilled when I realized it was him. "Venali," I hissed.

He smirked, but quickly removed it. "You shouldn't be unescorted right now. Where are the others?"

"They were just nearby," I said with a scowl and looked around for my other mates.

He held out his arm, and I set my hand on his forearm. "Let me escort you to your seat."

"Do you think someone will try to hurt me here?" I asked with a frown.

He sighed softly. "I would hope not, but people will do many things to accomplish their goals."

He stopped at the throne they had built for me, and I sat on it. With a bow, he stepped to the side and took up his role as guard. His hand rested on his sword, and he looked especially menacing today. He'd worn his hair up, so his scars were more prominent.

Durlan walked up the podium and bowed to me. "Your Majesty."

"Durlan, is it about to start?" I asked.

He shook his head. "We have some time. Do you need anything?"

"Some food and drink would be nice," I said and then frowned when I realized there was only one seat on the podium, mine. "Where will you be sitting?"

"We will be standing behind you," Durlan explained.

I scowled. "You're supposed to be my equals, remember? You need chairs."

"Who will be on your right?" Durlan asked with an arched brow.

Dammit. I knew what he was getting at. Even if I said they were my equals, people would view whoever was on my right as the leader, as someone who had more authority and power than the others.

"What if you sat in a line behind me?" I asked.

"We wouldn't be your equals if we were behind you," Venali whispered.

"You're not my equals if you're standing behind me either," I muttered and then sighed. There didn't seem to be a way to win this. "Wouldn't you prefer to sit anyway? You'll be standing for hours."

"If we can't stand for a day, we have no business being your guards, let alone your mates," Venali scoffed.

"That means I won't be allowed to touch you guys all day?" I asked softly, my mood plummeting.

Durlan dropped to one knee before me. "I'm sorry, my queen."

"I understand," I whispered and leaned back on my throne.

Durlan stood and took a step back to stand behind me.

The stands filled up as people took their seats to prepare for the tournament. At the far end of the arena, a group of men gathered. They looked like warriors, which meant they had to be the contenders for warlord. I couldn't tell from this far away how much power they had, though.

"Venali," I called softly.

He stepped up next to me and knelt on one knee. "Yes, Your Majesty?"

"What are their power levels? Are there any on par with yours?"

"We've told you before that there are none in Minloa who are as powerful as us."

"Then are they really capable enough or strong enough to be warlords?" I asked.

He was quiet a moment, as though he were choosing his words carefully before answering. "They may not be as powerful as us, but that doesn't mean that they aren't capable of being warlord. I doubt they will ever have to fight enemies as strong as us, and if they do happen to find an enemy as strong as us, they can team up and defeat it together."

"Is that something you've done?" I asked and turned to face him.

He nodded. "A few times over the last several hundred years."

That surprised me. What type of beings had they fought that required them to team up?

"I'm going to get your refreshments," Durlan said. He paused beside me a moment and asked, "Do you want anything else?"

"A kiss?" I requested.

He smirked, bent on one knee, picked up my hand, and kissed the back of it. "As my queen wishes."

I glowered at him.

He laughed as he walked away.

"You're my mates. Why can't we kiss?" I grumbled to Venali.

"Soon, beautiful," he whispered and then stood back up and took his position behind me.

"Where is Ryul?" I asked. He'd been avoiding me the last few days, and I wasn't sure why.

"I'm not certain," Venali answered.

"Why is he avoiding me?" I asked softly.

"It is not my place to discuss what he is or is not doing," Venali said.

I turned and stared at him. "You're taking his side! You like him more than me."

He chuckled and shook his head. "I assure you, that I do not like any of the others as I like you."

"I hope not," I mumbled, and turned back around.

"Have you tried talking to him?" he asked.

"How can I talk to him when he avoids me?" I grumbled.

He didn't respond to that.

Another hour passed, and then all of my mates made their way to the platform and stood behind me.

As I'd expected, Ryul didn't meet my gaze when he came to stand with the others.

Amrynn set a small table beside me, and then Durlan set the food and drink he'd brought for me on it.

"Thank you," I said and smiled at the two of them.

They took their spots, and we let silence descend upon us for a couple of minutes.

Finally, Venali stepped forward, drew power, and then projected his voice over the whole area. "People of Minloa! The Tournament is about to begin."

People scurried to their seats, once there, they all stared at me and began whispering to each other.

"Who is she?"

"Is that the queen?"

"She does look like the paintings I've seen."

Venali waited until everyone was seated, stepped back, and motioned for Durlan.

Durlan stepped forward and projected his voice as well. "People of Minloa, it is my honor to present to you, Queen Elara."

I stood, and people cheered. Smiling, I waved to them. Durlan had taught me last night how to project my voice like they did. I used it now. "Fight well. I need the strongest in Minloa to take up the mantle of warlord. You will be protecting your sectors, and will be advisors to my mates."

"Fighters, prepare yourselves," Durlan announced.

I sat back down and got comfortable.

CHAPTER 10
ELARA

THE CONTENDERS WALKED to the front of the arena, standing before me in a row. There were at least thirty of them ranging in age.

As one, they bowed to me.

That was going to take some getting used to.

"Your first test will be hand to hand combat with no magic," Durlan announced.

Venali walked from the podium and hopped over the fence into the arena.

"What is he doing?" I hissed softly.

"He's going to fight them," Amrynn answered me.

"They can't defeat him," I grumbled. "He'll knock out all of them and we won't have any contenders left for warlord."

Amrynn chuckled softly. "He's going to go easy on them. The last ten standing will continue on to the next round."

I picked up a piece of fruit and chewed on it.

"This is a free for all," Durlan explained. "You will be fighting each other, as well as Venali. The last ten left standing will proceed to round two."

Venali turned to face me, bowed, and when he stood, gave me a wink.

"He'd better make this interesting and not knock them all out in the first minute," I mumbled.

Kydrus chuckled. "You underestimate how much Venali enjoys this type of thing."

The contenders had moved apart, giving themselves space to fight. One of them, a tall man with black hair and dark eyes, stared at me. His eyes were intrigued, but there was something else in his expression, too.

Pain?

"Anyone know him?" Ryul asked.

"Oh, you do speak," I whispered. "I thought you'd gone mute."

Ryul growled softly.

"And, he is not the only one staring at me," I added. "So, I don't think you need to be worried."

"I've never seen him before," Amrynn answered Ryul, completely ignoring my comments.

"He's masking his power," Kydrus said.

"I can't get a read on him at all," Ryul said. "Keep an eye on him."

The man in question turned from me to look at Ryul and the others behind me, his brows furrowing in anger, and eyes darkening, and then he turned to face the other contenders.

As much as I wanted to dismiss Ryul's worry, there was something different about that man. Something familiar.

Venali moved off to the side, surveying the group and looking excited. It was rare that I saw him this excited and my heart fluttered in response.

Durlan waited a moment while the crowd grew quiet, and then he said, "Begin!"

The man who'd been staring at me dodged an attack from a man on his right, hit the man on the head, and the man fell to the ground and didn't get back up.

"Um, are they allowed to kill each other?" I asked, my heart beating faster.

"He's not dead, just knocked out," Ryul said.

"Well, that's good," I whispered.

I had expected the fight to be chaos, but there were a handful of men who were simply waiting on the outside, knocking out anyone who tried to fight them, and watching the fights inside.

The crowd roared and cheered. Some cheered for specific contenders, while others just cheered for the fighting.

Venali had yet to fight anyone, watching like the other men on the outside.

The men in the center, gathered in a small cluster, were engaged in pure chaos.

"Groups," Kydrus said.

"Interesting," Amrynn whispered.

"What?" I asked, having no idea what they were talking about.

"There are two groups of three in the middle. Each trio is working together to fight people off," Kydrus said, leaning closer to me.

Now that he pointed it out, I could see the groups as they stood back to back, fighting off attackers.

Venali finally joined the fight, leaping into the very center, knocking out one of the trios. I'd expected him to smile as he fought, but he looked stoic. The only excitement lay in his eyes.

The men who had been waiting on the outside joined the fray, knocking people out quickly, one after the next.

"Did they plan this?" I asked.

"Possibly," Kydrus said. "Or, they just know they're stronger and were biding their time so they didn't have to fight as many people."

The outliers made it to the middle where Venali and one of the trios were still fighting other contenders.

The numbers finally dwindled to ten, not counting Venali.

Durlan shouted, "Halt!"

Everyone froze, except the man who'd been staring at me. He took a step closer to Venali, who watched him calmly. The man said something to Venali.

Venali's face contorted in rage, and he lunged for the man.

"Venali!" I yelled.

Venali froze, but his eyes did not stray from the man.

The man teleported from the arena to stand before me.

Kydrus, Amrynn, and Ryul moved as one, their swords drawn and pressed to the man's throat.

The man looked extremely calm for someone who had three blades ready to cut his head off.

"State your business," Kydrus growled.

"You're hiding yourself still. Why do you pretend to be a weak shell? Have you fallen so far?" the man asked while staring at me.

"Who are you?" I asked, standing and drawing my own sword.

"You'd know if you hadn't put a wall up between us," he said and growled softly. "Was that your idea or one of theirs?" he asked, looking at Kydrus and Ryul who stood in front of him.

My eyes widened, and I lowered my sword. "No."

"What's the meaning of this ruse?" the man asked.

"Kydrus. Ryul. You two escort him to the house. Durlan and Amrynn, continue the tournament. We'll return shortly," I ordered.

"Your Majesty," Amrynn growled. "I don't think—"

I looked at him and said, "Do as I order."

Amrynn bowed. "Yes, Your Majesty."

"You three, let's go," I ordered, and headed down from the platform, towards the house.

Kydrus walked behind me, then the man, and then Ryul bringing up the rear to guard Kydrus's back as he protected me.

People murmured as we left.

"Are they going to punish him?"

"They're probably going to kill him," another person said.

I refrained from commenting. They didn't need to know what was going on.

Once inside the house, I led them to the living room, and stood in front of the fireplace, looking down at the logs. "Sit," I ordered them.

I heard shuffling and then silence.

I turned around and faced the man. "Drop your glamour."

He smirked. "I don't know what you're talking about."

"Drop your glamour," I ordered him.

Ryul and Kydrus tensed.

"Drop the wall between us," he replied, staring defiantly

back at me.

I stepped forward, pressing my sword to his throat. "Drop your glamour!"

He didn't even flinch. His eyes never left mine. "You won't kill me. You can't kill me," he whispered.

My arm shook. He was right.

"She can't, but we can," Ryul said.

"Oh, brother. You've fallen so far as well," the man said. He looked at Ryul a moment, and then faced me again. "Come on, let me in. Why are you hiding? Why are you keeping me out?" He set his hands on my hips, and pulled me forward, onto his lap. "Let me in."

His touch made me gasp, and broke a bit of the wall I'd built up between us.

"It's too soon," I whispered. "You weren't supposed to be here. You were supposed to wait for me to come."

"You blocked me. I worried you were in danger," he whispered.

"Who is this guy?" Ryul growled.

He dropped his glamour, his appearance shifting slightly. He still looked basically the same, but his eyes were pitch black, and he had longer than normal canines, even for a fae.

"Unseelie!" Ryul barked, lunging forward.

Kydrus lunged towards me, but I held up my hands, stopping them.

"What is your name?" I asked softly.

"Myrin," he answered, pulling me closer, so I straddled his lap.

I dropped the wall between us, and our bond snapped into place, connecting us instantly. His feelings and the connection were so strong, that I couldn't believe I'd been able to keep him out for so long. I gasped, arching into him, and then leaned forward to kiss him.

My sixth mate.

"What is going on?" Ryul asked.

Myrin pulled back from our kiss, but held me against his chest. He turned, and pointed at his neck. "I'm Myrin, Amara's mate."

I growled. "Don't say that name. My name is Elara."

Myrin's brows furrowed as he searched my face. "I don't understand."

"An Unseelie is your mate," Kydrus whispered.

"No. This is unacceptable," Ryul snapped, drawing his sword.

Myrin stood, pushing me behind him. "Stand down," he ordered Ryul.

I stepped in front of Myrin, glaring at Ryul. "You will not hurt him. He is my mate. I understand that this is difficult for you to handle, but it is the truth."

Ryul turned his glare on me. "You knew? You knew you had an Unseelie as a mate?"

"I suspected," I said. "I blocked them as soon as I realized I had more mates. I did it so quickly that I didn't get much of a sense for them." I turned around to face Myrin. "How did you find me?"

He smirked and rested his hand on my cheek. "I will always find you. I am your consort. You are mine. Even with the wall you'd put up between us, I could find you."

"You remember our prior life?" I asked, my eyes wide.

"You don't?" he asked, eyebrows furrowed.

"She's refusing to accept who she is," Ryul explained. "We aren't allowed to even say her true name."

"That's why you're sick," Myrin realized.

I bristled. "I'm not sick."

"You are. I can smell it on you and sense it through our bond," he said. The hand on my cheek slid back behind my neck, and he tilted my head up to look at him. "Why won't you accept who you are?"

"I'm Elara, former slave and Queen of Minloa. I am not a goddess," I whispered.

"Former slave? What are you talking about?" Myrin asked, his fury sparking flames within his eyes.

"There's a lot you need to be told," Kydrus said, finally speaking for the first time.

"Clearly," Myrin mumbled. He bent forward, pressed his forehead to mine, and the coolness of his skin against mine made me exhale in joy. The heat continued to leave my body until the fog in my head cleared, and I felt almost normal again. Myrin leaned back and asked, "Better?"

I threw my arms around his neck, stood on tiptoe, and kissed him. "You're amazing," I whispered.

Ryul growled.

"You need to go back to the tournament," Kydrus told me. "And he can't go back out there looking like this."

"Like what? An Unseelie?" Myrin asked, snarling.

"Yes," Kydrus answered with zero hostility.

"You are so ignorant," Myrin said and sighed. "The Seelie have fallen so far."

"Watch it," Ryul threatened.

"Ryul," I snapped. "You will not fight Myrin. He is my mate, whether you like it or not."

Ryul snarled and stormed out of the house, slamming the door closed behind him.

"He'll come around," Kydrus assured me. "This is a lot to take in."

"Not for you," I noticed.

"Amrynn had a feeling one of the reasons you wanted to go to the Unseelie was because you had a mate there," he said.

"No. That's not the reason at all." I frowned and shook my head.

"You were planning to go see the Unseelie, to their den, without me?" Myrin asked, scowling.

I smiled and chuckled nervously. "Maybe."

He growled and lowered himself until his face was level with mine. "You never go to the Unseelie without me present. Do you understand?"

"Why were you in the tournament? Why not just come find me?" I asked instead of answering him.

"I wanted a chance to see you and your other consorts," he admitted.

"What did you say to Venali?" I asked. I'd been curious about it because Venali rarely lost his composure.

"That he was much weaker in this new body than he had been before," Myrin said, smiling.

That would do it.

"Put a different glamour on," I ordered him. "We need to go back to the tournament. You're going to have to sit in the crowd with the other people. Tonight, we can talk more."

Myrin bowed, and when he stood, he had on new glamour that made him look like a different Seelie fae. "I am but here to serve my queen."

The idea of him serving me in other ways had me clenching my legs together. "Let's go," I ordered them. "I have warlords to pick."

CHAPTER II
ELARA

Venali stood on the platform with his sword drawn when we approached, his eyes locked on Myrin.

I walked straight up to Venali, and it took him a moment to remember where we were.

He dropped to one knee and bowed his head.

"You are not to hurt him," I whispered. "We will discuss this after the tournament. Do you understand?"

"Yes, my queen," Venali whispered.

"I love you," I whispered even softer.

Venali's lip twitched as he fought to hide his smile. "I love you, too."

"Do me a favor? Go find Ryul and make sure he doesn't kill anyone."

Venali's eyes widened, but he just bobbed his head and stood. "As you wish."

I sat in my chair, and my mates took their spots. I glanced at Durlan. "What is the status?"

"They are on a thirty minute break," Durlan answered. "When the break is over, we will move to the second round."

"How much more time on their break?" I asked. The nine remaining men looked rested. The people were talking and laughing and it seemed like some were even making bets.

"Two minutes," Durlan answered.

I nodded and grabbed my cup to drink from. I started to raise it to my lips, but smelled something foul coming from it.

Poison.

I wasn't sure how I knew or could smell it, but I had no doubt.

I tossed the drink out, being sure not to react in anyway. "Amrynn," I called.

He came to my side. "Here."

"Can you get me a different drink? The last one wasn't appetizing."

His eyes widened as he understood what I was trying to say.

Durlan growled softly, but his expression didn't change.

"I'll get you new refreshments, Your Majesty," Amrynn said, grabbed the cup from my hands, and picked up the tray of food as well. He took them to the house.

"I was here the entire time," Durlan whispered.

"Then we need to be especially careful," I whispered.

"Keep your drink in your lap," Kydrus ordered me.

"Very well," I said softly.

Knowing someone had tried to kill me should have upset me, but it only made me sad. Whoever this person, or persons, were, they wanted to kill me without even getting to know me. It hurt a bit.

Amrynn returned with new food and drink, and moved the table closer to me.

I kept the cup in my lap, and drank from it slowly.

"It is time for our next round," Durlan announced. "This round, we will test your magic."

This, I was anxious to see.

Amrynn jumped into the arena.

"You will be paired up and must use your magic against each other," Durlan explained. "No killing is allowed."

"There's an odd number," I whispered to myself.

"That's why Amrynn is there," Kydrus whispered to me.

"No one's going to be able to defeat him," I muttered.

"No, but he will know if the person's attacks are strong enough to pass the test and move forward," Kydrus replied.

I wasn't so sure I agreed with that, but I sat quietly as I waited for them to start the second round.

The contenders spread out across the arena, split into pairs.

I watched, curious which of them would continue on.

"Ready!" Durlan yelled and waited a moment before continuing, "Begin."

One of the contenders in the middle used a lightning spell that struck the man across from him.

The lightning struck the man, but the man did not react. He didn't even flinch. He just lifted his hand, and a bolt of blue light sped from his palm to the other man. The lightning user fell, his body twitching as he lay on the ground.

"One down," Kydrus said quietly, leaning toward me.

Only, that wasn't right. By the time I looked over at the other contenders, three more were down.

The man facing Amrynn used a spell I'd never seen before. It created a dark mist that moved into a humanoid shape.

I gripped the arms of my chair.

Amrynn raised his hand, and the man stopped, letting his spell dissolve. "Pass," Amrynn said, and walked back to us.

"What was that?" I hissed.

"You don't want to know," Kydrus whispered. "I haven't seen someone use that power in at least a decade."

Amrynn knelt by me. "He's going to be a warlord."

"You're sure?" I asked.

Amrynn nodded once and then stood. "I'm certain."

"Those remaining, prepare for the final test," Durlan called.

I looked at him. "More? But there are five."

"Trust me, Your Majesty," he replied, smiling.

I nodded once and tapped my finger on the arm of my chair. What could the final test be?

CHAPTER 12
VENALI

Ryul stood in the forest, gaze fixed on the canopy of leaves overhead. "She continues to withhold information from us," he said as I approached.

"She does what she thinks is right," I said. "We need to show her that we are truly her equals and deserving of her confidence."

He growled. "An Unseelie? Of all the circumstances to come up, that was not one I expected to have to accept."

"I don't like it either, but she is certain. If she is certain, then we must trust her."

He lowered his head to meet my gaze. "She is dying, still. It has slowed, but she is very weak."

"The more of her mates she has with her, the safer she will be," I offered.

"You've changed," he snarled.

"You haven't," I countered.

"She—"

"Has been trying to talk to you, but you are avoiding her. Tell me how that helps anyone?" I interrupted him.

"I can't temper my anger when I feel her dying. I just want to shake her and scream until she starts acting like the damn goddess she is."

"You should know by now that approach won't work with Elara," I said and shook my head.

"Since when did you become the reasonable one of the two of us?" he asked through clenched teeth.

"Since I got my memories back and remembered what it felt like not only to be parted from her while she was on another world, but also when she died," I said, rubbing my chest to ease the ache there. "I will not push her away. I will not do anything that will make her *want* to push me away."

"You're coddling her." Ryul growled. "I don't want to lose her either, but letting her kill herself and letting that Unseelie—"

"She is our queen, our goddess. She decides what we do. I cannot control her any more than I can control the future. And, that is how it should be. No one should control her. If you cannot accept that, if you cannot accept one of her mates, you will be left behind. I suggest you adapt. You don't have to like it, I know I don't, but we have to accept it and do what we can to keep her safe."

He snarled, showing me his canines, and then sighed and lowered his head. "I get it."

I nodded and turned. "Good. I'm going back to stand beside her. Hopefully, you'll do the same."

I understood Ryul's frustration. I did. But I refused to push Elara away.

Back at the tournament, I paused by her newest mate.

He glanced at me, but returned to watching the arena.

"Can you protect her in the Unseelie realm?" I asked softly, staring straight ahead.

"She's truly planning to go there?" he asked.

I nodded once.

"I can, but I will need your help. I'm not like Ryul, I can admit my faults, especially when it comes to her safety," he said softly.

"They don't have all of their memories back," I informed him.

He turned to look at me, smirking. "You do, though."

It wasn't a question, but I nodded anyway. "Most."

He chuckled softly.

"She is dying," I whispered. "Pushing her will not help."

"She's afraid," he said with a frown.

I nodded again. "This has been a rough life for her."

"Will you tell me what I've missed?" he asked, brow furrowed.

I let out a slow breath. "After this. Meet me in the house once we are finished."

He nodded, and I left to stand behind Elara on the podium.

"All is well?" she asked while staring at the remaining five men.

"Yes, Your Majesty," I answered, keeping my gaze fixed on her while I bowed slightly.

Her shoulders relaxed and she released an audible breath. "Good."

If Ryul didn't pull his head from his ass soon, I would beat him until it came out. She had enough to worry about. He didn't need to add to it.

Kydrus glanced at me before facing forward again. I could sense his anger from just that brief look.

It seemed I would have backup for beating Ryul.

CHAPTER 13
ELARA

Durlan knelt beside me and whispered, "You need to go into the arena."

"Why?" I asked without moving.

"The final test is them bowing to you," he explained.

I sighed, but did as he asked. When Venali tried to follow me, I raised my hand, stopping him and the others.

"Alone," I whispered.

Kydrus's lip twitched, but my mates stayed on the podium.

I hopped over the fence, and smoothed down my dress once on the ground. Hand on the hilt of my sword, I walked to the candidates.

They stood in a line, watching me, some with curiosity, but one with a darkness boiling in his eyes I did not like.

They'd bowed to me at the beginning, so this shouldn't be any different, right?

I stopped, drew my sword, and said, "To become my warlords, you must bow to me. Bow to me now, before all these witnesses."

The one Amrynn had faced with the strange power bowed immediately.

Another bowed.

And then the one glaring at me spit on the ground.

I cleared the distance between us in the blink of an eye, and pressed my sword to his throat.

His eyes widened, and his mouth dropped open.

"What is this?" I asked him.

"I...I will not bow to a slave," he said, though his conviction was not conveyed in his tone.

Oh. Well, that certainly made this easier.

"You owned slaves?" I asked.

"Your owner should have beaten you more," he hissed and raised his hand to hit me.

I grabbed his arm, twisted it up behind his back like Venali had taught me, kicked the back of his knees, and then rested my sword atop his shoulder, the blade touching the side of his throat.

"All witness his testimony of slavery? An act punishable by death?" I asked the crowd.

"Witnessed," hundreds of voices rang out.

My mates gripped their swords, but held their places.

"Your punishment is death," I told him, and then slid my sword across his throat, and stepped back to let his body fall.

His blood sprayed my face and arms.

Yuck.

One of the four behind me held out a handkerchief.

I took it with a smile. "Thank you."

After wiping off the blood, I turned to the crowd. "Behind me stand your new warlords. I expect them to be treated as well as the previous ones."

I started to walk from the arena, but someone in the audience asked, "How do we know you're really the queen?"

People stepped back from the man who had spoken.

I walked to stand before him, only the fence between us. Lifting my hand, I gripped the moon, and pulled it from the sky. Thankfully, today was a clear day and one the moon could be seen even while the sun was out.

People screamed, some cheered, and the man teetered.

I held the moon in my hand, the size of a grapefruit, and asked, "Any other questions?"

The man shook his head from side to side.

I smiled and threw the moon back up to its rightful place. "Good." With a wide smile, I walked from the arena, through the crowd which parted for me, and to the house.

Once inside the living room, I fainted on the floor.

Worth it.

CHAPTER 14
ELARA

"You've always been dramatic, but that was over the top, even for you," Myrin said softly.

I opened my eyes, surprised to find us alone in the house. "I didn't want to waste time," I said.

"Beautiful one, why must you persist on causing me panic?" he asked and picked me up.

He carried me down the hallway.

"Where are you taking me?" I asked.

"To shower. You still have blood on you," he said and growled.

I knew he was my mate, but I only remembered snippets of him, and I did not know who he was in this life.

"I will not touch you or look at you, if that is your wish," he whispered.

"I..."

"Our bond has always been stronger than the others. It will take you some time to get used to. I will try not to pry into your feelings, if possible. I wish you would accept yourself, but this is your life and you must do what you think is right. I support you in whatever you do."

"So, Unseelie aren't evil creatures? I had suspected as much from the book I read, but it's difficult to release years of brainwashing so quickly."

He pushed open the bathroom with his foot and grumbled incoherently beneath his breath.

Once he set me down, I turned him to face me, and asked, "What of us?"

He scowled. "I don't understand."

"This is not my original body. Does it..." I bit my lip and looked at his chest. "Does it not entice you?"

"It doesn't matter what body you inhibit, Amara. You are my mate and I will worship you in whatever form you take. Though, I'd prefer if it were at least female forms."

For some reason, when he used that name, it didn't bother me.

He began unlacing my dress, his fingers moving expertly. "When I saw you today, it felt like I breathed for the first time. It was like I was sleep walking, and your presence woke me from my long slumber."

"I am not her," I whispered.

He helped me slide the dress off, and then looked me over, taking his eyes from my toes to my head. "Your body is not the same, but here..." he rested his hand on my breastbone. "...it is the same."

Heat stirred, and my core ached.

He stepped closer, dipped his head beside my ear and asked, "May I worship you, my queen?"

I didn't know what he meant, but nodded.

He placed a kiss on my neck, picked me up and lay me

down on my back, and then began kissing every inch of me, including my fingertips and toes. He held himself over me, his body hovering over mine, but not touching. "You are gorgeous. You have forgotten that. My job is to remind you." He dropped his head and drew my nipple into his mouth.

I arched up with a gasp.

He released me only to take my other nipple into his mouth. Then, he peppered kisses down the center of my body until he got to my aching bundle of nerves. He paused, looked up at me, and said, "Let me show you what it means to be worshipped." His tongue swept over me, and he didn't stop until I was mush beneath his mouth.

His fingers massaged my inner legs, and then he plunged his tongue into my core.

"I will kill anyone who tries to take such sweet nectar from me," he whispered, licking me again and moaning.

"Please," I begged.

"Do not beg, Amara. You are the goddess. Order. I am your faithful consort. Tell me what you want."

"I want to be one with you," I said.

He removed his clothes, lay atop me so that our skin touched as much as possible, and then he slid inside of me, filling me up not only literally, but also emotionally.

He pumped into me, whispering praises the entire time.

Our bond solidified even more, and for a moment, there was only Myrin and I.

I screamed his name as I orgasmed, and he kissed me deeply.

I flipped us over, riding him and moaning loudly with each movement.

He rested his hands on my hips, stroking his thumbs on

my hip bones. "I am your tool, Goddess. I will shape myself to your needs."

I peaked again, gripping his chest as the wave crashed over me.

He took over, pumping up into me to keep the orgasm going.

"No one can compare to you. You are perfect."

He moved faster, his eyes on me the entire time.

"Myrin," I moaned.

"Elara!" he yelled as he orgasmed, his body shuddering its final movements.

He leaned forward, placing kisses all across my chest.

"Now you need a shower, too," I chuckled.

He withdrew from me and said, "I suppose I do."

CHAPTER 15

KYDRUS

Elara spent a lot of time with Myrin the few days following the tournament. We traveled to the castle, and she often opted to spend her evenings with him. Not that she refused to see us, or ignored us, but she definitely had a closer bond to Myrin, despite knowing him for the least amount of time.

I tried not to let it bother me, but seeing her so affectionate with an Unseelie unsettled me. He didn't appear to be evil, which further unnerved me. Everything we had been taught was wrong. Every prejudice we had against the Unseelie. Well, maybe not *every* prejudice.

"She's remembering more," Amrynn whispered to me as we watched her sparring with Venali.

I nodded, studying her movements. "It seems like Myrin broke her walls down a bit."

"Do you remember everything?" he asked, glancing at me before his eyes returned to our mate.

"No. Venali seems to remember the most, next to Myrin who knows everything."

"We should talk to him tonight," Amrynn said, crossing his arms over his chest, his eyes never left Elara's form. "Learn what we can."

I nodded my agreement.

Then Elara stumbled, falling to her knees. When Venali reached out towards her, she held her hand up to ward him off. "I'm fine."

Only, she wasn't. Her goddess powers were eating at her. I clenched my jaw to push down my anxiety.

"What's going on?" Myrin asked as he came to our side.

"She's sparring," Amrynn answered.

"We'd like to talk to you tonight," I told him. "To learn as much as we can from you."

Myrin tilted his head and looked at me with an eyebrow raised. "You're calmer this lifetime."

"I don't know if that's a compliment or not," I muttered.

He smiled. "It's a compliment. You were rather rash last time." His smile disappeared. "It was part of what got you killed."

My eyes widened. "I thought Amara and her mates just disappeared."

He laughed bitterly and looked up at the sky. "If only that were true."

"We only remember snippets," Amrynn admitted to him. "How can you remember it all?"

Myrin shrugged. "I don't know. When she accepted you five as mates, the memories came back to me, and I felt her." He looked at Elara, scowling. "I felt her sickness, and started my journey to find her."

"You've been good for her," I said, as much as it hurt me

to admit it. "She's accepting herself a bit more now that you're here."

"When she finds her final mate, she'll accept herself again," Myrin said, but the set of his jaw made me think that was just his hope.

"Who is her last mate?" Amrynn asked.

Myrin smirked and shook his head. "Nope. I am not ruining that surprise."

She cried out and fell again, and Myrin walked to her. She tried to push him away, but he squatted down and pressed his forehead to her. Her eyes fluttered closed, and then the painful twist to her features relaxed.

The knife's edge of pain I felt down our bond dulled. It was strange to feel another's pain or temperament. It was also strange to be able to communicate telepathically with the others. We'd closed down the bonds, since we didn't need to communicate currently, and most of us didn't want our thoughts shared with the others.

Myrin stood and walked back to us. "After she falls asleep, we'll meet. Make sure Ryul comes. He needs to hear what I have to say even if he doesn't like me."

I wanted to say Ryul would come around to Myrin, but I wasn't sure. Ryul's hatred towards Myrin was more than just him being an Unseelie, but I couldn't understand what it was.

Amrynn nodded, and Myrin left.

"What are we going to do about Ryul?" Amrynn asked.

I sighed and ran a hand through my hair. "No idea."

"We should talk to Durlan," I suggested.

After another long look at our mate, we turned and walked to Durlan's office on the far side of the castle. He sat behind the desk, reading something and scowling.

"You look like you're having fun," I said as I sat in a chair in front of his desk.

Amrynn shut the door and sat beside me.

Durlan sighed and tossed the paper on his desk. "Not in the slightest." He looked at us and scowled. "What's going on?"

"We came to talk about Ryul," I explained.

Durlan leaned back in his chair, rubbing his eyes before running his hand down his face. "He's the most stubborn of us. Even more stubborn than Venali, which I didn't think was possible."

"He refuses to accept Myrin," Amrynn said. "If we aren't united, that jeopardizes Elara."

"Any idea what we can do?" I asked, leaning forward in my seat.

Durlan shook his head. "I think Ryul feels threatened by Myrin. He's only been here a week, yet she acts as close to him as she does Amrynn. Ryul was her best friend, or so he thought, and now his status is uncertain."

"He's her mate, that won't change." I frowned.

"No, but her attention has not been given to him," Durlan said.

"He keeps pushing her away and hiding. How is she supposed to give him attention?" I asked with a growl, hands fisting.

"He wants her to seek him out," Amrynn whispered and sighed. "I see."

"Why? To prove she still cares? He would know her feeling for him if he let his walls down a bit. He's causing her pain by ignoring her. I've seen the way she looks at him when he walks by without acknowledging her," I said and then took a deep breath and let it out slowly.

"He is acting childish," Durlan said with a nod. "But we can't call him on it or it will only exacerbate things."

"We've asked Myrin to speak to us tonight, to tell us what he can about our prior lives and Amara. He agreed to meet us after Elara falls asleep," I said.

Durlan smiled. "Good. I've been meaning to talk to him."

"We need to convince Ryul to come," Amrynn said.

Durlan shrugged. "We'll just tell him he has to come."

"We could tie him up, if he refuses," I said with a chuckle.

"He'll use his powers to deceive us," Amrynn said, raising a brow.

"True," I muttered.

"I'll talk to him," Durlan said and stood. "You two need to go work with the new warlords. They need a crash course on their duties. I think Elara is growing antsy to leave."

I'd sensed it as well.

Amrynn and I stood.

"See you tonight," I told Durlan and headed to find the new warlords. As much as I hated teaching, we needed to be sure we left the realm in good hands.

I just hoped we returned before anything happened.

CHAPTER 16
AMRYNN

"Elara is asleep," Myrin announced as he closed her bedroom door.

"Magically or naturally?" I asked with a smirk.

He chuckled. "Naturally."

"We're meeting in the war room," I said to him, turning down the hallway.

Part of me rebelled at leaving Elara alone, unprotected, but we wouldn't be far from her, and she should, hopefully sleep the entire time we were gone.

"She'll be fine," Myrin said softly, smirking at me.

I let out an audible sigh. "I know."

He patted my shoulder while chuckling.

We entered the war room to find the four others gathered and sitting in chairs around the giant table in the center, where a map of the realm sat.

Myrin had a seat in Elara's chair so we could all see him.

I sat beside Ryul, in case I needed to restrain him.

"So, none of you have all of your memories?" Myrin asked.

We shook our heads.

"Venali has the most," Kydrus gestured towards him.

"Any of you remember our deaths?" Myrin asked, his voice dropping a bit.

We all shook our heads again.

"Let's start from the beginning," he said. "Amara chose to rule on this planet instead of from the stars. She said she couldn't understand the strife of her children if she wasn't here to see them. Being here weakened her, but since she could draw on the power of the stars, it didn't matter. We were her equals, able to make decisions even when she wasn't with us. Things were going well, until darkness came from another universe. It fell in Minloa, and Amara tried to stop it, but it was beyond her powers."

"Darkness from another universe? You mean a creature?" Kydrus asked.

Myrin shook his head. "No. It was a dark substance on a meteorite that landed here. A fae touched it, and it changed him. Amara didn't want to destroy the man, so she kept an eye on him. He did some things that were not quite moral, but nothing truly evil. She was conflicted. On one hand, he hadn't really done anything to deserve death, but on the other hand, he had spread the darkness to a few more."

"It spread through touch?" Durlan asked.

Myrin nodded. "Obviously, that's not the case anymore, but it was then."

"You touched it," Ryul guessed.

Myrin smirked. "Yes. I thought I was immune, but I was wrong."

"It changed you?" I asked.

He sighed and created a black flame. "Yes and no. I

gained new powers, but my moral compass did not change. I was still the same. Amara could see that, but some of us couldn't." He looked pointedly at Ryul. "You tried to kill me."

Ryul's expression was carefully neutral.

"Amara made it a rule that we could not kill each other, unless our life was in danger. You became enraged, convinced I would kill Amara if given the chance," Myrin continued. "It took decades for you to realize that I wasn't a threat. Decades that prevented us from seeing the true danger building on Anderelle, our planet."

"True danger?" I asked.

"I don't want to ruin the surprise," he said, smirking, "but there are several reasons Elara wants to go on this journey. This true danger was the reason we all died. Amara sacrificed herself to try to save us, but her sacrifice was in vain. We all died, and she somehow saved our souls, so we could be reincarnated."

I crossed my arms over my chest. "I thought you were going to tell us everything?"

Myrin shrugged. "It's not my fault you can't access your memories."

"Why is Elara so drawn to you?" Ryul asked, his face still a courtly mask of nothing.

Kydrus and I leaned forward, anxious to hear this answer as well.

"I was her first mate. The last to die. And, the one who drew her back when she let the stars seduce her."

"I've done that," I whispered. "Though, the method I used won't work now."

"Tell me about her past in this life," Myrin ordered.

I glanced at Kydrus and Durlan.

Durlan sighed. "Fine, I'll tell him."

He told Myrin everything, and throughout it Myrin grew angrier and angrier.

Finished, Durlan sat back and watched Myrin.

Myrin closed his eyes, drew in a big breath, and let it out slowly. When he opened his eyes, the anger was gone. "That explains why she finds it so difficult to accept that she is a goddess."

"What's going on?" Elara asked, rubbing her eyes as she entered the room.

We froze, uncertain how to answer her.

"Mate meeting," Ryul said. "We didn't want to wake you, so we came here."

She sat on his lap, curling up her legs so she fit against his chest, and closed her eyes. "Okay. I'll just sleep while you talk."

Ryul's eyes widened, and then slowly he wrapped his arms around her. The mask fell, and we all saw the sadness there.

"How much time do you need to train the new warlords?" Myrin asked.

"A week," Kydrus answered. "They're pretty smart, and have been watching us, so they know most of our duties."

"We will set off as soon as they are ready," Myrin said.

"You're acting like you are in charge," Ryul said with a frown. "Who appointed you leader?"

Elara stirred, and then relaxed.

"She did," Myrin said, looking at Elara. "As first mate, I was dubbed leader."

Ryul growled softly.

Elara bolted upright, her head swiveling from side to side. "What?"

Ryul tugged her back against his chest. "Sorry. Nothing is wrong. Back to sleep."

She frowned, looked at each of us, and then slumped against him again.

Myrin sighed softly. "What do I have to do? Your distrust fractures us and puts Elara at risk."

Ryul looked down at Elara, scowling. "I don't know."

At least he was being honest.

"If you can't accept Myrin, you will put Elara at risk on our trip. If that's the case, it may be better for you to stay behind," Durlan said. His words were soft, but the conviction in his eyes wasn't.

Ryul glared at him. "I'm not staying behind."

"Then deal with the shit in your head, stop pushing Elara away, and accept Myrin," Kydrus growled and stood. "I tire of your childishness."

Had Ryul not been holding Elara, I was certain he would have taken a swing at Kydrus. As it was, he stood, cradling her, and left.

"That either fixed things or made it worse," I muttered.

Myrin shrugged. "When it comes to him, you never know."

CHAPTER 17
ELARA

Ryul woke me with kisses along my collar bone.

"This is one of my favorite ways to be woken," I said, opening my eyes to look at him.

His mouth crashed into mine, his need burning like a living flame, and engulfing me with it.

"I'm sorry I've been an idiot lately," he whispered as he removed my clothes and kissed my body. "I've been pouting and acting like a child because I felt like you were replacing me with Myrin."

I spread my legs, letting him dive into me, arching up and gripping his back as he buried himself in me. I was often wet enough for them to slide in without foreplay, and right now I was very happy for that.

"I'm sorry. I wasn't trying to ignore you or spend less time with you," I said.

He slid out of me and then slowly slid back in, moaning as he fully entered me. He stilled and looked down into my eyes. "I love you, Elara."

I smiled and pulled him down for a kiss. "I love you, too. Now, make me scream."

He sat up, smiling wide, and did as I ordered, making me scream several times.

When he had finished, we cuddled a moment before going to the shower, where he cleaned me.

"I'm sorry I was neglecting you," I whispered as I soaped up his body. "No one will ever replace you. I need you just as much as I need the others."

"You trust Myrin?" he asked softly.

"With my life," I said and nodded.

"Then I trust him, too."

We finished our shower, and the light was back in Ryul's eyes again.

I linked our fingers together and smiled up at him. "Let's get food. I'm hungry."

He raised our joined hands and kissed the back of mine. "Lead the way and I will follow. To the ends of the universe or farther."

"I'd rather stay in this galaxy," I said with a chuckle.

The four new warlords sat with my other mates, but quickly rose from their seats to bow.

"Please sit," I said, sitting between Amrynn and Durlan. "I'm hungry."

Durlan pushed a plate of food to me. "Here, my queen."

I kissed his cheek and dug in.

"Communication between the four of you is the most important thing," Kydrus told the warlords. "There will be times that you need one or more of the other's help. Don't be ashamed to ask for aid."

"Be sure to squash any challengers quickly," Venali said.

"And punish those who break the rules," Kydrus added.

"If they view you as weak, they won't listen to you," Venali told them.

"But that doesn't mean rule with an iron fist," I pipped up. "Durlan was loved by his people for being kind and compassionate, but they also knew if needed, he would crush them."

Everyone turned to look at me.

"What?" I asked. "I learned things while in your sectors."

Most of my mates smirked at me, while the warlords looked curious.

"What's on my itinerary today?" I asked, stretching my arms above my head.

"You are free today," Durlan said.

I dropped my arms and gaped at him. "What?"

Venali chuckled.

Durlan smiled. "You have no itinerary today. You are free to do as you wish."

I frowned down at the table.

Do what I wished? What did I want to do?

I hadn't had free time since becoming their mate.

"We will continue our discussion elsewhere," Kydrus instructed the warlords. He dropped a kiss on my cheek before walking out with the warlords following him.

"You look upset," Myrin said, eyebrow raised.

"I don't know what I should do today."

"What did you do before you found out who you are?" Ryul asked.

I blushed and said, "Nothing."

"Would you like to have a picnic somewhere?" Ryul asked.

That did sound nice.

"What about a swim in the ocean, followed by a picnic?" Myrin asked.

I hadn't been to the ocean in a long time.

"The ocean sounds nice, as does a picnic," I said.

"Great, I'll get the picnic ready," Ryul said and left.

"I don't have a swimsuit," I mumbled.

"You could just swim naked," Amrynn whispered in my ear and kissed my neck.

I shivered and arched my head to give him better access to my neck. "People will see us," I countered.

"Ryul can use a spell to hide us," Myrin said and then kissed the other side of my neck.

"If you don't stop, we aren't going to make it to the ocean," I groaned. Why was I saying this? Why was I stopping them?

Amrynn rested his hand against my forehead with a scowl. "I think she's sick."

"Clearly. I've never heard of her turning down sex before," Myrin said.

"Especially not with several of us at once," Durlan added.

"I just really want to go to the ocean," I said with a sigh.

"We've got plenty of time. It's still really early," Amrynn said, picked me up out of the chair, and crushed his mouth to mine.

I wrapped my arms and legs around him, holding on as he walked.

He walked without opening his eyes, and our kiss never stopped.

The door opened, and then he tossed me onto my bed.

I yelped, shocked at the sudden air time.

"How are we going to do this?" Myrin asked. "I've yet to participate in a group session."

"I think we should take turns," Durlan said. "That way it draws out her pleasure."

I licked my lips, watching as they stripped their shirts off. "I like that idea."

Amrynn grabbed his shirt from the floor where he'd just thrown it, tore a strip off, and then tied it around my eyes.

"What?" I gasped.

Hands touched me, removing my clothes, and then my body was repositioned so that I was on my back with my legs spread, and rump near the end of the bed.

The hands disappeared, and just as I was about to whine, a mouth covered my most sensitive part.

I gasped and grabbed the sheets.

"I think she likes that," Amrynn said off to my left.

The mouth sucked and then they used their tongue, driving me to the point of pleasure, and then stopping and moving away.

I cried out and reached for the person, but they were gone.

Hands slid up my legs, then I felt the head of a dick pressed against my entrance.

I tried to move, to get them to enter me, but they backed away.

I huffed and crossed my arms.

"No hiding those beautiful breasts," Myrin ordered me from my left.

Wait, hadn't Amrynn just been on my left?

"Stop teasing me then." I pouted.

The head was back, and then they pushed it inside.

"Yes," I moaned, arching up.

Whoever it was grabbed my hips, and began a fast rhythm that had me screaming in seconds.

Normally, they switched positions, but whoever was with me now just held the same position. Which was totally fine with me since they were hitting the right spot, and I had four orgasms before they found their release.

That person withdrew and then a new person replaced them.

This one flipped me onto my stomach, pulling me backwards until my feet touched the floor, while I still laid on the bed. I eagerly waited for them to enter me, but instead was greeted with a face between my legs. They licked and sucked and pleasured me until I peaked and cried out as I fell over the cliff of ecstasy.

Then, they pushed into me, and found a perfect rhythm of pleasure.

I was the luckiest woman in the world.

CHAPTER 18
ELARA

THE BEACH WAS COLDER than I remembered, but I didn't let it bother me. We laid out a blanket, and ate lunch. We kept the food inside the basket unless we were eating it, so we wouldn't have to deal with the birds flying around the beach.

Leaning back against Venali, I closed my eyes and relaxed as the sun warmed me, yet the wind chilled me.

"This is nice," I whispered. "We should do this more often."

"We will try to set aside time for this," Durlan said with a smile. "Though, it will be difficult once we leave on our trip."

I cringed. There was so much to do on this trip. So much danger and so much that could go wrong.

"There are going to be some problems when we go to the Unseelie," Myrin said. "You're going to have to allow me to do most of the talking. Ryul, you're going to have to keep your mouth closed."

Ryul grumbled, but didn't argue.

"Could you teleport us to the Unseelie?" I asked Myrin.

It hadn't been an option before, since the rest of us had never been there.

He shook his head. "I can't teleport. No Unseelie can."

Really? Why not?

"That sucks," Ryul said.

Myrin chuckled. "Yeah."

"So, two of us will have to double up anytime we teleport then," Durlan said.

Myrin frowned. "Two of you?"

"I can't teleport on this planet," I explained.

"She can teleport to other planets, but no small jumps," Amrynn added.

"Interesting," Myrin murmured, looking out over the ocean.

We lapsed into silence, and I enjoyed the calm, quiet time with my men. Soon, things would be hectic and danger-ous, and I didn't know how we would fare.

As the sun dipped lower, I stood and brushed my clothes off. "We should head back."

They agreed and packed everything up. Then we walked to the castle and to our separate rooms. Ryul followed me to my room, and we showered together, but for once there were no other activities in the shower.

It was almost dinner time, so we headed to the dining room.

Kydrus pulled me into a deep kiss, making a smile spread across my face when he released me.

"What was that for?" I asked, brushing some of his hair back behind his ear.

"Do I need a reason to kiss the most beautiful woman in the galaxy?" he asked, arching a brow.

"Only the galaxy?" I asked, sticking my lip out in a pout.

He chuckled and kissed me again. "In all of the universes in all of the timelines that ever existed."

"Better," I whispered, smiling wide.

"I am here to serve, my queen," he whispered, and then nipped my earlobe.

I groaned and arched up into him. "No teasing me before dinner."

"Shall I wait until dinner or do I need to wait until after dinner?" he asked, his husky voice next to my ear and his words soft enough that only I heard them.

"He's just jealous that he didn't get to join in earlier," Amrynn said from the chair where he sat.

Kydrus released me and took his seat. "I'm not jealous."

"Disappointed," Amrynn amended.

"Broody," Ryul said.

"Pouting," Myrin said.

We all laughed and Kydrus smiled. "You all would feel the same."

Myrin nodded. "True."

I sat at the head of the table. "How was your training?"

Kydrus smiled. "They're doing well. I have no doubt they'll be ready."

"Good," I said.

"So, are you going to tell us everything?" Myrin asked.

"Did you know that a female red-toed lizard can run as fast as an owl can fly?" I asked, picked up my napkin and set it in my lap without looking at any of them.

"That was an amazing topic shift." Durlan applauded. "Any other Seelie would have no idea how to respond because they wouldn't be able to ignore your question, and yet you completely ignored theirs."

I beamed with pride.

"Yes, and now answer our question," Ryul said.

"No," I answered, folding my arms on top of the table. "Now, let's talk about supplies."

"We need to know what we're doing before we can determine what supplies we need," Kydrus said.

"Supplies for extreme heat, supplies for extreme cold, and supplies for in between," I answered.

"How far and how long are we traveling?" Myrin asked.

"Far and at least a month," I answered.

"Farther than the Unseelie's island?" Ryul asked.

I nodded. "Much farther than Eltare."

All of the men turned to look at each other, and I was certain they were communicating telepathically with their new link. I wanted to peek into their conversation, but that would open me to my last mate, and I was trying very hard to keep him out.

They turned to look at me as one, which was rather creepy.

"Another continent?" Durlan asked.

I nodded.

Ryul cursed beneath his breath.

"So, we need a sturdy ship," Kydrus commented.

"I'll reach out to the harbor. I have contacts there," Amrynn said.

"I hate boats," Ryul whispered.

"Can you swim?" I asked him, tilting my head to the side. When we were kids, he hadn't been able to.

He didn't respond, just stared at the tabletop.

"We need to teach you to swim," Amrynn said. "The last thing we need is for you to drown during a sea storm."

"Sea storm?" he asked and gulped.

Amrynn nodded. "They're notoriously bad between continents in the open waters."

"Your food is served," a waiter said as he and three others brought out trays of food and set them on the table.

I still wasn't used to the fact that we had employees in the castle who did this type of thing. It was nice, and super convenient, but, recently, I had been cooking food on a campfire more than having others cook for me.

"She's brooding," Durlan said.

Kydrus looked at me. "You'll get used to it soon. If you hadn't been so scared of me before, you could have eaten with me and been a little more used to others preparing your food."

"It's not my fault you're scary," I mumbled, spooning some vegetables onto my plate.

"He's scary?" Myrin asked, eyebrows raised. "No offense, Kydrus."

"None taken," Kydrus said with a smirk.

"He was the most powerful being around me," I argued. "He could kill me with a snap of his fingers. Why wouldn't I have been scared of him as a poor little slave?"

"Former slave," Kydrus amended.

"You know what I mean," I mumbled around the food in my mouth.

"I still can't believe you were a slave as a child," Myrin whispered. "Your powers or your memories should have at least presented themselves enough to save you from such a fate."

"Tell them that," I muttered.

"At least you're not as skittish now," Amrynn whispered.

Kydrus scoffed. "You're telling me. Even when I was trying to heal her, she flinched or acted like I was about to hit her. I thought she'd had an abusive lover."

"None of my lovers were ever abusive," I whispered before taking another bite of food. I felt their eyes on me, so I looked up. "What?"

"Lovers? You had lovers before us?" Amrynn asked.

Whoops.

"Yes."

I focused on my food, ignoring the stares which were still focused on me.

"How many?"

I sighed and asked, "Do you really want to discuss this? Do you want to tell me your numbers?" I looked at Kydrus. "I saw the number of women who went in and out of your house." I turned to Ryul. "You told me you slept with others." I looked at Amrynn. "Everyone talked about the revolving door into your house."

Each looked like they'd eaten something sour.

"Whoa," Myrin said, his eyes wide. "You cheated on her?"

"We didn't know she existed," Venali argued.

"Wait? You didn't sleep with anyone?" Ryul asked Myrin.

Myrin shook his head. "I never touched a woman until her."

"Liar," Venali whispered.

Myrin scowled. "I'm telling the truth."

"Did women ever touch you?" Venali asked.

This was so not a dinner conversation I wanted to have.

"Do we really need to discuss this?" I asked.

"No, I didn't let any other women touch me," Myrin answered. "I knew I had a mate, and I waited for her even if I didn't know who she was."

Now I was a little skeptical. "You're pretty good for someone who never had practice."

All eyes turned to me, most with anger.

I shrugged unapologetically. "Just being honest. He's good."

Myrin smirked, the smugness shining from him like a beacon. "I appreciate the compliment. No, I never slept with anyone or did anything with anyone else."

"Fine, no women, what about men?" Amrynn asked.

Myrin laughed loudly while shaking his head. "No. I don't swing that way."

I looked at everyone. "Do any of you?" Not that I had a problem if they were attracted to men as well. Though, I had no desire to share them.

"No," they all answered simultaneously.

"Can we change the subject?" I begged.

"Who did you sleep with?" Kydrus asked.

My eyes widened. "No. No way. Nope."

"What?" Amrynn asked.

"If I tell you, you'll probably go kill them or something," I said, shaking my head.

"No, we wouldn't," Amrynn said.

"You wouldn't," Venali whispered.

Ryul snarled and nodded.

I pointed at them. "See?"

"How many?" Durlan asked.

"More than one," I answered.

"More than five?" Kydrus asked.

"No," I answered.

"More than three?" Myrin asked.

"I'm done with this questioning," I told them. "It was before you guys. Before I remembered I was a princess. Well before I remembered I was...me."

"So, you admit you are more than a princess?" Ryul asked with a smirk.

I pushed my chair back and stood. "I admit that you're an ass." I left the room, snagging a roll on my way out, and went to the war room. "Pushy, assholes," I growled. I locked the door behind me, so the guys couldn't bust inside.

I reached beneath my dad's desk, hitting the secret button, and waited as the secret compartment opened. Inside lay a rolled-up piece of parchment. I spread it out on the desk, put a few items on the corners to hold it open, and looked at the map. It was the only map in existence, that I knew of, that showed the entire planet and the continents.

I took another piece of parchment, one I'd stowed in the same compartment, and resumed copying. I wanted to take my replica with me on the journey, so I could keep track of where we went. I added markers to a few places, and tried to figure out what course we would take. Which was the best way to visit the places I needed to visit.

"Elara," Ryul called through the door as he tried the locked handle. "Please let me in."

I rolled the parchment up, and put it back in the compartment, then walked and unlocked the door. I opened it and scowled up at him. "What?"

"I'm sorry," he whispered.

He did look apologetic.

"You're forgiven," I said and tried to close the door.

He looked over my head into the room. "Why are you hiding in here?"

"I'm busy," I said and pushed him. "Shoo."

He gawked at me. "Shoo? Did you just shoo me?"

"I did. Now, shoo," I said and pushed his chest.

He caught my hand, and his eyes glimmered with pain. "I wish you would trust us. We may argue with you, but we are your consorts. Your mates. We are here for you."

"Soon," I whispered. "Soon, I'll be able to fully trust you."

His eyes glimmered brighter, the pain sharper. "What can I do?"

"Leave me for now," I said. "And tell the others to leave me for the rest of the night."

He sighed and nodded. "Alright."

He released my hand, and it pained me to make him leave, but I needed to work this out on my own. Once I was sure he was gone, I locked the door behind me, and returned to the desk, pulling the parchment pieces out again.

"This is why you're hiding?" Myrin asked.

I yelped, and spun to push him in the chest.

He chuckled and caught my hands. "Didn't know I was here?"

"No," I gasped. "How did you get in? I thought you couldn't teleport?"

"I can't teleport, but I can faze through things, like the wall," he said. He walked to the desk and looked over the maps. "We're visiting all of the continents?"

"You're not supposed to see this," I mumbled.

"Elara, you may be able to keep them in the dark, but

don't forget that I remember our prior lives. I remember you and everything about your personality. You're slightly different now, but the core of you is the same."

"Then you know that I need to rule over all of the continents, to unite them," I whispered.

"I wasn't sure if you were going to do that since you weren't accepting who you are," he said.

"I'm not going as...*her*. I'm going as Elara," I snapped.

He scowled, which made him no less handsome. Why was I so drawn to him? Of all my mates, I felt the strongest connection to him.

"I am most worried about the Unseelie," I whispered. "They've been demonized for centuries by these idiots."

"Bitterness runs rampant among the Unseelie." Myrin traced his finger from our current place to the island. "This will be our easiest journey." He traced from the island to the next continent, which had a lot of ocean between it. "This will be our most difficult."

"If I die..." I whispered, but couldn't finish my sentence.

Myrin closed the distance between us and stared down into my eyes. "You will not."

"If I do, please protect them. They are still unbalanced."

"They will be whole, when you are," he whispered. "Sweet, beautiful woman. You drive me crazy."

I smirked. "In a good way?"

I expected him to smile, but he did not. "Sometimes."

Scowling, I stepped away from him. "I'd like some time alone."

"Time to scheme," he whispered from right behind me.

"Call it what you will," I snapped. "But I'd like you to leave."

He kissed my cheek, and then disappeared.

I huffed and sat in the chair behind the desk. He irked me, but mostly because he was right.

Resuming my task, I added place markers, and mapped out our journey. The journey alone would take us a month, roundtrip. I wasn't sure how long each stop on our trip would take.

I was going to have to convince the leaders of the continents to let me lead them. To do that, I would need to use my powers. I wasn't ready for that yet. I needed to see the Unseelie first. I wasn't as nervous now that Myrin was here. I'd been scared what he might do to my other mates. Him coming with his full memory was not what I'd expected. I was grateful, though. At least I wouldn't have to worry about him when we visited the Unseelie. Now, he would be at my side.

I'd almost laughed when he had told Ryul he would have to keep his mouth shut. Myrin was right, though. Ryul had to learn to rein in his temper. And, when to be quiet and let others handle it.

Of them all, he was the most immature and unseasoned. He'd stayed in the castle most of the time, so he didn't have the experience that the others did when it came to battle. I hoped this trip would help him.

Finished with my work, I put the maps back in the secret compartment, and then returned to my room. Just a few more days before we left. A few more days of calm before the storm of my desire to unify our planet.

CHAPTER 19

DURLAN

ELARA WAS HIDING information from us. Some of it wasn't vital, she was allowed her secrets like we were allowed ours. But I had a feeling that some of it was very important and knowing it would help us.

"You're scowling," Myrin said as he entered my room. He shut the door behind him, and then sat in one of the chairs around the small dining table I'd had brought in.

"An expression I make often these past few months," I said and sat across from him. I folded my hands in my lap. "What can I do for you?"

"She's going much farther than I thought. This isn't just a trip to the Unseelie."

I nodded. "I know. She said we were going to other continents."

His eyes widened. "She did?"

"Yes."

He ran a hand through his hair. "Did she tell you anything else?"

"No, but it seems you may know more."

He smirked. "I know quite a bit more, but I'm not sure what I can tell you without getting in trouble with our queen."

"Enough that we won't be in danger?"

He tossed his head back and laughed. "Durlan, when it comes to our queen, our mate, you must know that everything she does will put us in danger."

I growled at him.

"I'm just saying, she likes to do things that are dangerous, and we, as her mates, go with her to protect her. She has a constant target on her back, and that has not changed in any of our lifetimes."

"You remember more than just our previous one?" I asked, leaning forward.

He waved his hand dismissively. "No, we've only had one before this."

Somehow, I didn't believe him, but I let that topic drop.

"You're worried, too," I said, seeing the tension in the corners of his eyes.

He sighed. "She's hurting every day that she doesn't accept who she is. She knows, but she won't accept it enough to release her powers. I don't know what to do to convince her to accept it. I am doing my best to keep her pain at bay, but soon it will overwhelm her."

"How soon will that happen?" I asked.

He shrugged. "A year. A month. Tomorrow. I have no idea. If she continues at the pace she is, most likely in a month."

"In a month, we should be on another continent," I whispered, looking off in the distance. What would that do?

Would she be seen as weak, and whatever goal she has there be negated?

"Exactly."

"So, we need to convince her to accept herself within a month," I said, chuckled, and shook my head. "Easy."

Myrin laughed, too. "Yeah. Nothing is easy for us."

"Or for her," I said. We might be hard on her, but it was only because we wanted her to be able to move on, beyond all the terrible shit she had had to endure.

"I think we should completely avoid the topic of Amara for the next two weeks at least," Myrin said. "Especially while we are in the Unseelie realm."

"Why? Wouldn't it be better if the Unseelie knew she was a goddess?"

He scoffed. "No."

"What should we expect when we go to the Unseelie?" I asked. I'd been wanting to discuss it with him for a while now.

"Anger. Resentment. Posturing. They're bitter at the way the Seelie treat them. The ignorance has made them hostile. If Ryul can't keep his mouth shut, and mouths off to one of them, he'll likely have to fight an Unseelie."

"And you don't think he can win that battle?"

Myrin shrugged. "Each Unseelie has unique powers, just like the Seelie. I have no idea who he might go up against."

"So, taping his mouth shut might help?" I asked with a smirk. I was joking, but if it came down to it, I would knock him out. I would not let him endanger Elara because he was green still. He might have been as old as us, but he did not have the experience that we had. He had never even been in a battle.

"Knowing him, he'll still flex on someone and end up causing a fight. We can't leave him behind, because we might need him if a fight does break out. There really is no good option." Myrin looked up at the ceiling. "I'm worried, Durlan. This is a feeling I'm not used to."

"Well, you better get used to it," I said.

He lowered his head to look at me again. "I'd like to tell you something about yourself. From our previous life."

I leaned forward expectantly. "Okay."

"You've always been the one who worries the most."

I sat back and rolled my eyes. "Really?"

He laughed. "Sorry. I do have something to tell you, though."

"Still waiting," I said and sighed.

"You were able to shield her. I don't know if you can do that now, but you were able to create magical barriers that prevented people from touching her or attacking her with magic. She has some magic that requires her to concentrate for a few moments before she can use it. You were able to shield her during those times, or when she was down and we weren't close to her. If you can't do that now, you should try. It was one of the only things that kept her alive as long as she was before."

A magical barrier? I'd heard of people doing that, but hadn't tried myself.

"I will work on that," I said.

He stood. "There's so much I wish I could tell you. Try to convince the others not to say anything to her about Amara, okay? It may help if we aren't pressuring her."

"You mean talk to Ryul," I said and smirked.

He nodded. "He and I won't ever get along, Durlan. No

matter what I do, he is predisposed to hate me. I wish it were different, but that's where we are at. We should all take that into consideration and be prepared for him to try to screw me over, which could screw us all over."

"I'll try to break him down. You have to realize that he was in this castle for hundreds of years, just waiting for Elara. He doesn't have the experience the rest of us do."

He nodded. "I hope you're able to break him down a bit. I don't want to hurt him, but Elara is my top priority."

I nodded. "Agreed."

We smiled at each other, and for the first time, I felt a deeper connection with him.

CHAPTER 20
MYRIN

THEY HAD no idea of the possible scenarios when we went to the Unseelie. I'd kept mostly to myself, but my power level was easily visible, so they'd still noticed me. I had seen first-hand the darkness and hostility brewing there. Their hate for the Seelie was unrivaled.

The fact that my mate was Seelie would cause a stir. Me, bringing other Seelie back with me, especially prior warlords, would upset a lot of them.

I was likely going to have to kill someone. Elara was likely going to have to kill someone, too. She might have to kill several people to get them to acknowledge that she was powerful and deserving of their respect.

The current monarch was a handful. I had no idea how they would react to Elara.

"Hey," Kydrus called.

I stopped, turning in the hallway I had been walking down. I didn't have a destination in mind, so I'd started aimlessly wandering the castle.

"What's up?" I asked.

He stopped in front of me, his eyes gleaming with mischief. "You should come out to the arena with me."

I scowled at him. "If you think you're going to beat me or—"

He rolled his eyes. "I'm not Ryul. No, Ryul and Venali are fighting. I think you should watch."

Seeing Ryul's fighting ability would be good.

"Okay," I said. I turned and headed in the opposite direction, Kydrus at my side.

"Did you sneak into her room?" Kydrus asked.

I chuckled. "Yes, but she kicked me out."

"Not surprising," he muttered.

We didn't talk as we walked the rest of the way to the arena. Once there, we sat on the fence to watch them.

Venali glanced over. He smirked, which caused the scars over his eyes to crinkle a moment, and then he turned back to Ryul. "No holding back. Magic allowed."

"If I use magic, you'll lose instantly," Ryul said. He brushed invisible dust off his shoulder.

So cocky.

"Try me," Venali said.

Ryul held his hand out, and Venali froze.

What was he seeing? Ryul could manipulate reality, so it could be anything.

Venali shook himself, and then took a swing at Ryul, barely missing his nose.

Ryul backed up, scowling. "What?"

"I didn't break your spell," Venali said, advancing and swinging at Ryul. "But I have spent enough time with you to be able to sense you wherever you are, even with your tricks."

"Maybe you should actually fight him," I suggested.

Ryul gave me a glare, anger making his eyes flare bright. He dropped his spell and attacked Venali.

Venali easily dodged the attacks, and swept his feet out from under him.

I had to hand it to the brute, even in this life he was quick.

Ryul glanced at me, saw my smirk, and growled. He waved his hand at Venali, and something drastic changed.

Venali froze again, but this time agony twisted his face. "Stop," he growled, his voice sounding strained.

Ryul punched Venali, knocking the big man back a step.

Venali had tears in his eyes, and he didn't even try to fight back.

"It's not real!" I yelled.

Ryul continued attacking Venali, landing blow after blow.

What could he be showing Venali that would make him stop like this? He knew it was fake. He knew it because he had started this match.

"Stop!" Venali roared.

Ryul stepped back and released his magic.

Venali fell to his knees and dropped his head forward. "You're a fucking prick."

"You said use my magic," Ryul said, but he didn't sound quite so smug anymore.

"What did he show you?" I asked Venali.

"Why don't you come and find out?" Ryul taunted.

Venali had gathered himself again, and I could see the anger brewing. I leapt down and jogged to stand in front of him. "Venali," I whispered.

Venali turned away. "I'm fine."

"Try me," I said, facing Ryul.

Ryul tilted his head to the side as he looked at me. "You want the same as I gave Venali?"

I nodded.

"You sure?" he asked. "You saw how he reacted."

"Show me," I growled.

Ryul snapped his fingers, and all around me was a battlefield. Dead Seelie and Unseelie covered the ground, their blood painting everything red. A few were still fighting, Venali, Kydrus, and Durlan among them. The enemy was one I had not seen before. They looked similar to us, but their teeth were not sharp. I spun around, and the sight before me made my heart stop. In the middle of it stood a man with a spear, and before him, on her back, lay Elara. Elara held up her hands and begged the man to spare her.

I held still.

This wasn't real. This was just an illusion.

Tears streamed down Elara's cheeks, mixing with blood that seeped from several wounds on her face. She was covered in wounds.

"Remove your bonds with your consorts," the man said. "And I might spare you."

"Anything. I'll do anything but that," she wept.

The man raised the spear and aimed it at her heart. "Then, die."

She screamed as the spear plunged into her chest. Her blood burst out in an arc.

My body ached to run to her. To kill the man.

I knew it wasn't real. But the pain I felt was.

"What's going on?" Elara asked.

The image shattered, and I turned to find her.

She stood, wrapped in Venali's arms, her eyes wide as she surveyed us.

"That's a great magic for when you know the person and their worst fear. But what if you don't know them?" I asked.

Ryul chuckled. "I don't need to know them personally. Everyone has fears. Plus, I don't have to show them something they fear. I can just change the area so they don't know where I am."

"Venali, fight him again," I said. "This time, no horrors."

I switched Venali places, picked Elara up in my arms, and carried her to the sidelines. I placed several kisses on her cheeks.

She was here. She was safe. She was not dead.

"What's wrong with you two?" Elara asked, snuggling her face into the crook of my neck.

"Ryul showed us you dying," I said.

She tensed. "What?"

"We asked him to use his magic to fight us." I nuzzled her and kissed her forehead.

"I'm not dead," she said and hugged me around the neck.

Venali faced Ryul. His fists were clenched and a red aura swirled around him. "Show me what other tricks you have."

"Is this necessary?" Elara asked and then yawned.

"You should go to sleep." I adjusted my hold on her so that I was fully supporting her weight, and then hopped up on the fence beside Kydrus.

"What did he show you?" Kydrus asked.

"Elara being killed by a weird man with dull teeth," I said.

"Humans," Elara gasped. "That's even more cruel than showing my death."

"Humans? The things that took you in their spaceship?" Now I really wanted to punch Ryul in the face. I could understand why Venali was so angry now.

"Yes," Elara said. "Ryul is rude."

I chuckled. "He did what he was supposed to do."

Venali and Ryul began fighting. At first, they fought hand to hand, neither excelling over the other, but then Ryul used his magic.

Quickly, Ryul darted away from Venali, moving to his back, left side.

Venali froze for a second, the aura around his hands glowed, and then he flung a fireball at Ryul.

Ryul ducked, avoiding the fire, his eyes wide.

Venali ran after Ryul, catching him with one, two, three... seven punches.

Ryul fell onto his back and raised his hand. "I yield."

"You're barely trying," Elara said.

"I'm tired," Ryul said, sitting up. "This isn't an actual battle, so I don't *have* to fight. I need some sleep."

Or, he was embarrassed by how pathetic his stamina was, and didn't want Elara to see.

"It is time to go to bed," I said. "We should all get some sleep."

Elara hopped out of my arms, walked to each of the guys to give them hugs, and then returned to me and held out her arms.

I picked her up and kissed her. "You're pretty damn perfect. I hope you know that."

She scoffed. "I'm far from perfect."

"Perfect for us. And that's all that matters."

CHAPTER 21
ELARA

WE LEFT AS SOON as the sun rose, headed away from the castle with no fanfare or goodbyes. Just me and my mates headed to meet people who despised us.

Easy peasy.

Durlan had a contact at the pier, and there was a boat waiting for us with no crew.

"How are we going to get there?" I asked.

"We can sail," Kydrus said, smirking.

"You can?" I asked, blinking.

"Just because we've been on land most of our lives doesn't mean we didn't learn how to sail," Kydrus said. "I'm offended."

I chuckled. "Sorry. I just can't picture you guys sailing."

Now that I said that, I was totally fantasizing about them shirtless and sailing a pirate ship.

"Stop thinking naughty thoughts," Myrin whispered in my ear as he passed by.

I shrugged unapologetically. "Not going to happen. You

guys are sexy and I enjoy thinking about naughty things with you all."

We boarded the ship, and the guys went into action to set sail. I had no idea what was going on, so I just sat on the railing in front of the steering wheel, and watched.

They were all working well together, even Ryul and Myrin. I was glad. The sooner Ryul accepted Myrin, the better. And the safer we would be. I didn't want discord between them to cause anyone to be injured or killed.

Myrin took the steering wheel and turned it, guiding the ship away from the dock and out into the open waters.

"We're going to be alright, right?" I asked Myrin softly.

"Yes, my goddess. We will be fine. You will be in danger, but I will ensure nothing harms you," he said.

I turned to look at him. "I meant all of us. I don't want something bad happening to you guys either."

He smiled, but was focused on steering, so he wasn't looking at me. "We will survive the Unseelie."

This was the shortest part of our journey, since Eltare was so close to our continent. I hopped down and walked to the front of the ship, looking out over the clear water which teemed with sea life.

"Don't lean too far forward," Ryul said with a frown and shake of his head. "You might fall in."

"The water is too cold for a swim. I won't fall in," I said and smiled back at him. He stood almost next to the center mast, his body tense, and fists clenched.

"You sure about this?" he asked, looking past me, in the direction of the island.

"Yes," I said immediately, facing the ocean again. "One hundred percent."

The anticipation and unknown were starting to get to me. There was so much that could go wrong.

"You remember to keep quiet," I said.

Ryul scoffed. "I know."

"I mean it," I said and turned to face him fully. "I don't want everyone being put in danger because you couldn't control your rage and your mouth."

He glared at me. "I'm not a child, Elara."

"No, but you're green compared to the others. And, your stubbornness caused part of our demise last lifetime," I said, striding towards him. It was a low blow, but one he needed to hear and be reminded of.

He sighed. "I know."

"Then strive to be better. Be the man I know you can be," I said, resting my hand on his cheek. "I love you."

"I love you, too," he said. He leaned into my hand, and then turned and kissed my palm. "I'll do better this lifetime. I just really wish I remembered our last one."

"You will, eventually," I said.

We sailed for several hours, but no one spoke aside from necessary call outs for our sailing. Everyone was lost in their own thoughts and try as I might, I became lost in mine as well. In the various ways the Unseelie could hurt my mates. In the various ways that I could screw up this meeting and my plans. I had to ensure everything went as planned. I had to make them agree to join us. It was imperative.

"Island!" Myrin called out.

I turned in the direction we were headed and smiled. There it was, the Unseelie island, Eltare. I was ready for this. Or, at least as ready as I could be in my current state.

Surprisingly, there was a dock with a few ships, and several people walking around.

The guys went to work getting the ship docked, and then we disembarked. Myrin took the lead, followed by the rest of us in a circle with me at the center.

People watched us and murmured to each other as we passed.

There were Seelie, Unseelie, and a few other races I couldn't place. They had to have come from some other continent.

"Stop gawking," Kydrus whispered. "You're making us fall behind."

I snapped my head back straight, and saw he was right, Myrin was far ahead.

We walked faster to catch up, and Myrin glanced back at us. "Mouths shut from here on out," he said.

Everyone nodded.

He led us down a wooden path, into some trees, and then stood before what looked like a castle gate, but there was no castle.

I wanted to ask, but he'd said to be silent, so I held my tongue.

Myrin placed his hand against the gate, closed his eyes, and whispered something.

The gate groaned.

Myrin backed up.

Slowly, the gate lowered. Through the opening, we could see a busy courtyard, full of Unseelie. Myrin exhaled. Then I watched in almost horror as he put on a mask of unfeeling confidence. He looked like an assassin. His eyes were so cold and soulless.

"Follow me," he ordered, even his voice was different.

He led us inside, head held high, and ignored everyone as if they didn't exist. We made it to the castle steps before guards intercepted us, their swords drawn.

Thankfully, none of my guys drew their swords.

"What's this?" one asked Myrin.

"Our monarch is going to want to speak to them," Myrin said.

"Why? Who are they?" the guard who had spoken asked.

"I'm not going to announce that here, where everyone can hear," Myrin snapped. "Get the royal advisor if you won't let us pass to speak to the monarch."

The same guard turned and whistled to another guard. That one walked into the castle.

The guards before us were tensed, ready to fight. Yet, I could sense no darkness from them.

The Unseelie weren't evil after all. We had been lied to. All of the Seelie were being lied to.

Why? Why make the Unseelie into monsters?

The castle doors opened, the guard who had left returned, and an older man came at his side.

The older man stopped before Myrin. "What's the meaning of this, Myrin? Why have you brought these *Seelie* here?"

He said Seelie like it was a curse word.

Myrin leaned close to his ear, whispering so softly that we couldn't hear.

The man's eyes widened, and he focused his attention on me.

Myrin continued to speak, but the man's gaze never left mine.

Finally, Myrin pulled back, blocking the man's view of me.

"Bring them in," the man said.

"Sir?" the guard asked.

"Did I stutter?" the man said and growled.

The guard stepped to the side, letting us pass.

Myrin headed up the stairs, and we followed.

I held my head high, not meeting anyone's eyes, but still trying to look regal. I would not appear submissive here. I would not, for a moment, let them think that I was to be walked over.

I admired the paintings on the hallway walls. There were several decorative vases and other items as well. It was all very pretty.

"Not what you expected, is it?" the man asked me.

I looked at him, but did not respond.

He took the hint, turning and pushing open double doors.

Inside, over a dozen people sat in rows before a throne, where a beautiful woman rested. Her hair was long, blood red, and she had a gorgeous crown a top her head.

She had long fingernails, painted the same blood red as her hair. She was paler than me, but her eyes were filled with a curious light that gave me hope. "What have you brought me, Myrin?" she asked in a lilting voice.

Myrin stopped at the base of the steps that led to the throne, and dropped to one knee.

I had to pinch myself to keep from snarling. I did not like him kneeling to her.

"I've brought you the Seelie Queen," Myrin said. "She's requested an audience, and I thought she might entertain you."

The queen smirked. "The Seelie Queen. What brought you here, to this cursed island?"

I stepped forward, the guys parting to let me through, and dipped my head in acknowledgement. "I'm Elara, Queen of Minloa. What may I call you?" I asked.

"I am Aerith, Queen of the Unseelie."

"I've requested an audience because it's become clear to me that the Unseelie have been demonized by previous rulers, and I wanted to set the record straight. I wanted a chance to meet with you to find out what you and your people are truly like," I said.

She tilted her head sideways as she looked at me, evaluating. "You speak the truth. How interesting. Well, Elara, we are not the evil, blood thirsty creatures the Seelie make us out to be. But, how can I prove that to you? Your people would just say that we played nice for your visit."

"They would come to see the truth, once we united and some of you returned to Minloa," I said.

Her eyes widened. "You would allow us back?"

"We're getting ahead of ourselves," I said with a smile. "Are you willing to allow us to stay here for a couple of days? To learn more about you?"

"How do I know you and your guards aren't here to attack us, or attempt to overthrow me?" Aerith asked, sitting up straight.

"I have the power to overthrow you," I said nonchalantly, with a shrug of my shoulders. "But my goal is to unite the continents, not kill."

She arched a brow and her lip twitched as she fought a snarl. "You are so sure of your ability to overthrow me. Don't you think that's a bit presumptuous since you do not know much about the Unseelie?"

I held out my hand towards Durlan. Myrin glanced at us, scowling.

I'd worked this plan out with Durlan in secret. I hadn't wanted anyone to know what I planned to do, except our strategist. He'd agreed to it.

Durlan opened his pack, and pulled out my crown, the one with the human planets in it, and then set it atop my head.

I turned to face Aerith and smiled. "I am *most* certain of my ability to defeat you in battle."

"Queen Elara—" Myrin growled.

I gave him a glare, and he shut up and took a step back.

Aerith stood, her eyes glowing turquoise. "You threaten me in my home?"

I shook my head. "I threaten no one. You seem ready to fight me, though. If you wish a demonstration, I am more than willing to oblige."

She growled and yelled, "Kill the men!"

My eyes widened. "Defend yourselves!" I snapped.

The guys drew their swords as guards encircled them, separating me from them.

"You seem so worried about these men. If I destroy them, perhaps you'll be less cocky," Aerith said.

I narrowed my eyes at Aerith. "If you harm my men, I will obliterate you from this planet. If you kill one of them, I will find you in every lifetime from here to eternity to torture and kill you. Do *not* touch my men."

Her eyes widened, but she held her tongue.

Her men attacked mine, swords clanging.

Myrin stayed rooted to his spot.

I felt pain in my arm, and turned to find Ryul bleeding from a cut just above his elbow.

I turned back to face Aerith, and more than anything wanted to make her cower.

Screw it all.

I dropped my barriers, claiming and admitting that I was Amara, Goddess and protector.

Power greater than anything I'd experienced before coursed through me, making my body glow.

Aerith's eyes widened, and she backed up a step, hedging towards hiding behind her throne.

"I am the goddess Amara. You will not harm my consorts!" I yelled. With a sweep of my hand, I knocked everyone except my consorts to the ground.

"You can't be," Aerith gasped from where she lay.

I walked to her, sword drawn, and pointed it at her throat. "I came here seeking hospitality, to try to unify our people. Instead, you took offense because I was more powerful than you. Are you so pathetic as to attack someone's allies in an attempt to weaken them? Clearly, you are. I do not approve. You will be better, Aerith, or I will find a new queen for my dark children."

She rolled into a bow before me. "Forgive me, Amara. I will be better."

I turned towards my guys, and my jaw dropped open. They were all glowing, their hair flying in an unseen wind, and eyes glowing.

"I remember," Ryul whispered.

"We all do," Venali said. He walked closer to me, and dropped to one knee, bowing his head. "My goddess."

The rest of my consorts came to me and bowed as well.

"Stand," I ordered everyone.

Everyone stood.

I turned and said, "The time for hiding is over. The Seelie will learn the truth about the Unseelie. It is time for us all to unite."

"Yes, Goddess," everyone said.

I turned to Myrin. "Escort me to chambers. I would like to talk with you all."

Myrin stood, and bowed at the waist. "Yes, my goddess."

"I'll talk with you more later," I told Aerith. "For now, tell your people that I am here, and I am unhappy."

I followed Myrin, head held high, and my crown thrumming with power.

Myrin led us to a large bedroom, and shut and locked the door behind him.

I glared at him. "If you ever bow to another person again, I will punish you."

He swallowed hard. "Yes, Amara."

"Now that we are here," I said, my chest tightening. I felt my body beginning to shake, and gulped. "Someone, catch me."

The power left my body as fast as it had come, and my strength went with it, causing my legs to give out, and I fell as my eyes rolled up into the back of my head.

CHAPTER 22
KYDRUS

AMARA'S EYES rolled up into the back of her head, her body stopped glowing, and she started to fall.

I leapt forward, catching her before she hit the ground, and cradled her in my lap. "Amara?" I asked, gently.

"What's wrong with her?" Venali asked.

"Her body isn't equipped to handle her goddess powers for too long," Ryul said. "She should wake in an hour or so."

I carried her to the bed and laid her down. Her hair fanned out around her like a halo, and she looked so peaceful as she slept.

She'd accepted who she was, unlocking our memories, but it seemed she would need to train her body to handle her powers.

I gently stroked her cheek.

"What was that back there, Durlan?" Myrin asked. "That was not what we had agreed to."

"Elara came to me last night and asked for me to keep her plan a secret. She said she was certain that the queen would not just accept her," Durlan said.

"She might have if she hadn't said she was stronger," Myrin growled.

"She wasn't wrong," I said softly. I spooned my body around Amara, or Elara, or whatever she wanted to be called. It was a bit cold in here, and I didn't want her to be uncomfortable.

"That's beside the point," Myrin said and threw his hands up in exasperation.

"Why are you upset? She accepted herself," Ryul said. "You should be happy."

Myrin looked at her sleeping beside me, and his face softened. "I am happy that she accepted herself, but she should not have kept such a plan a secret from me."

"You scared her when you prepared to come into the Unseelie court," I said.

Myrin's brows furrowed. "What?"

"When you closed off, became the aloof and cold blooded Unseelie you'd pretended to be all along, it scared her for a moment."

Myrin's brows furrowed more, but he said nothing.

"What's our plan?" Ryul asked. "Now that she's revealed who she is, it changes things."

"Not much," Durlan said.

She stirred beneath me, groaning, and her brows pinching.

I stroked her face from temple to jawline, and pressed a light kiss to the center of her forehead.

She relaxed, letting out an audible sigh, and stilled again.

I hadn't realized that the others had frozen during the moment until I turned towards them.

"This might make our trip easier," Durlan said. "They aren't likely to argue with a goddess about uniting."

"They will put up very little resistance," Venali said.

"I can't believe Aerith was going to have us killed," I whispered.

"She was close to killing everyone in the room," Durlan said.

We didn't need a name to know who he was talking about.

"For now, we stay together and protect her. I'm not sure what the others will think about her Seelie form," Durlan said. "She needs to be protected at all costs."

That was something everyone agreed on.

I would not fail my goddess, my love, again. I would not let her die.

CHAPTER 23
ELARA

I woke sweaty and thirsty.

"Water?" I requested weakly.

One of my consorts helped me sit up.

I opened my eyes, but it was pitch black in the room.

"Here," Kydrus said and a glass was pressed against my lips.

I grabbed the glass from him and gulped it down. Once I'd had my fill, I let the glass drop to my lap and asked, "Can we turn the light on?"

The lights came on, and I winced, covering my eyes with my hands.

"Sorry, there's no dimming ability," Ryul said.

I let my hands fall and looked at my guys. They weren't glowing anymore, but they still looked different. Godly somehow.

"What happened?" I asked.

"What do you remember?" Durlan asked.

"Fainting in the room," I said.

"You've been asleep since then," Kydrus said. "You slept for at least three hours."

I looked down at my arms. "I'm not a goddess still." I didn't want to say anything to them, but I wasn't sure I was fully Amara after all. There still felt like a separation between us.

"It seems your body can't handle you releasing your goddess powers for too long. You'll have to train to increase your stamina," Venali said.

I looked over at Myrin who hadn't spoken. "You're mad I withheld my plan from you."

"Irritated, but not mad," he said. He climbed out of the covers so he could sit in front of me. "But you accepted yourself, and that is well worth any irritation."

"I thought I would take on my goddess form permanently when I accepted it," I said. My brows furrowed in frustration. Why hadn't I become a full goddess?

"Is that why you wouldn't accept it before?" Myrin asked. I nodded.

"What do you want us to call you?" Kydrus asked.

That was a tough question. I was Amara, but I was also Elara. Both parts existed within me.

"Elara when in this form," I said.

"How do you feel?" Durlan asked.

"Fine. I'm mostly baffled I still have this form."

"You're beautiful no matter what form you take," Ryul said.

I leaned around Kydrus, so I could see Ryul, and smiled wide. "Thank you."

"What's the plan?" Myrin asked.

I sighed and fell back on the bed, looking up at the ceiling. "I don't know. I was fairly certain I would end up having to kill the monarch here, but I've decided to be merciful."

"You were getting ready to kill everyone," Durlan said.

I scowled. "Ryul was injured. I warned her, and she didn't stop the attack."

Ryul chuckled. "It was just a flesh wound."

I rolled my eyes.

"The people are going to want to see you," Myrin said. "In your goddess form."

I nodded. "Let's hope I can summon it at will." And that I didn't have to hold it for long.

"We should get more sleep," Durlan said. "I have a feeling tomorrow is going to be a long day."

The guys climbed back into their positions, and I rolled on to my side, laying my head on Kydrus's chest. Venali wrapped himself along my back.

Despite knowing I should sleep, it would not come.

Something was wrong with me. I wasn't sure what it was, but I needed to fix it. Fast.

My last consort tugged on our bond.

Closing my eyes, I focused on our bond and sent a single thought to him, "Soon."

The tugging stopped, but I could sense his irritation.

He was too far for me to worry about right now. After we left the Unseelie, I would seek him out.

For now, I would focus on the tasks at hand.

Aerith bowed to me as we entered the courtyard. She'd gathered as many of the Unseelie as she could.

I'd been able to take my goddess form, so I stood before them, glowing and looking badass with my crown atop my head.

"It is time for the Unseelie to come out of the shadows. It is time the Seelie learned the truth about you. We will not be divided. We will be united, and coexist together. It may take them time, but they will learn. After my journey, I will return to take volunteers back to the mainland to live there. You have a month to decide who among you is willing to go."

I turned and entered the castle, making long strides, but not long enough that it was obvious I was hurrying.

My consorts surrounded me, stern expressions on their faces to keep anyone who might want to talk to me away.

Fatigue pressed on me like a giant weight. My breathing became rougher, and I tripped.

Amrynn was right there with an arm out, somehow making it look like I just took his arm instead of tripping.

Myrin shut the door, and I collapsed in Amrynn's arms.

Durlan took my crown and placed it on the table. He inspected me with a scowl. "This doesn't make sense. You can command the cosmos, but you can't use your powers in this body?"

"No idea," I gasped. I lay limp in Amrynn's arms, my heart hammering like a caged bird.

"Drink some water." Kydrus held out a mug of water, and I gratefully accepted, gulping it down in two swallows.

"Do you need to do anything else before we head to our next destination?" Durlan asked.

Ringing started in my ears, and I felt hot and fuzzy. My mouth opened, but I couldn't make it speak.

"She's going to pass out," Amrynn said.

Durlan started using his healing magic on me, but this was beyond even him.

The world went dark, and I wondered if this was my punishment for holding back for too long.

CHAPTER 24

AMRYNN

"We should leave when it's dark," I said, still holding my sleeping queen. It had been two hours since she fainted, and while I could have put her on the bed, I preferred to have her in my arms where I could confirm she was breathing.

"That would look really suspect," Myrin said. "It may undermine what we're trying to accomplish."

"She needs to speak to Aerith once more before she leaves," Durlan said. "We'll have to wait until tomorrow. She'll speak to Aerith, we'll get on the ship, and then she'll likely faint and sleep for the first part of our journey."

Fainting so much couldn't be good for her health. Wasn't there anyway to help her body acclimate faster?

Someone knocked on the door, and all of our heads swiveled towards it.

Venali growled softly.

I carried Elara to the bed, laying with her so it looked like we were both asleep. Kydrus climbed on with us, laying on her other side.

Venali opened the door. "What?"

"Would Goddess Amara be willing to come eat with us?" a soft-spoken male asked.

"As you can see, she is taking a nap with two of her consorts," Venali said. "Perhaps another time."

"Queen Aerith was quite insistent." I could hear him fidgeting from here.

"I'll go," Elara said and sat up. She aimed a smile at the door. "I enjoy being in this form. It helps me learn more about my people."

Well, that was one way to handle the situation.

"I'll let her know you'll be joining us." The man hurried away with shuffling steps that meant an injured leg.

"Elara," Myrin growled.

"It's true. I wanted to be reincarnated in one of these forms so I could experience the pain and pleasure that my people faced. I hadn't planned to experience quite so much pain, but it was good. Besides, it will make me seem more empathetic and like a most understanding goddess," Elara said. She turned and looked down at me. "Why are you sleeping?"

I smirked. "We were pretending when the man came to speak to you. We weren't sure what they were going to want."

She returned my smirk, and then bent and pressed her soft, delectable lips to mine.

I wanted to devour her, taste every inch of her, but now was not the time.

She turned and kissed Kydrus as well, and then stood from the bed and stretched. "I don't think I have anything to wear."

"Just wear what you currently are," I said. "It will further the point that you wanted to live like them."

She smiled. "Okay."

"Well, I guess we're going to dinner," I said.

"Food!" Venali yelled.

CHAPTER 25

ELARA

My FATIGUE WAS GONE, but having to be completely unconscious for several hours was not ideal. It put me at a disadvantage, and put my consorts in danger.

"What can I do to stop from fainting?" I asked Ryul.

"We need to have you use your powers for just a few moments and then release them. We'll have you increase the time little by little until you'll be able to hold it for long periods," he said.

His eyes glowed as he spoke, and I got distracted by them, stumbling a step.

"You're drooling," Myrin whispered in my ear.

"It's not fair," I said, turning to face him.

He arched a brow. "What isn't?"

"You guys are all..." I waved my hand, unsure how to explain it.

"All what?" Myrin asked, smirking.

"Hot!" I snapped. "You look all godly and gorgeous."

All of them laughed.

"I'm glad you're all amused," I mumbled. I folded my

arms across my chest and ignored them all as we continued down the hallway. Why did this place have such long hallways?

We finally made it to the dining hall, and two Unseelie guards stood in front of the doors.

The guards stared at me without moving.

"I was invited," I said. "Please, step aside."

"You were invited, but not your consorts," the guard on the left said.

I stepped forward, getting right up in the guard's face. "My consorts come with me. Now, move or I will have you moved."

His lip twitched in the beginning of a snarl.

Before he could move, Myrin was there, grabbing the guard and throwing him down the hallway.

Venali grabbed the other guard at the same time and tossed him to the side.

The guards leapt up, but realizing they were outnumbered, they held their place.

Venali and Myrin opened the doors for me, bowing as I passed.

"Such considerate consorts," I said. The smile on my face was smug and satisfied.

Hundreds of Unseelie filled the dining hall. At the front on a raised dais sat Aerith.

Everyone turned to look at me.

I felt my guys step up behind me, which gave me more confidence.

I slapped a smile on my face, and walked through the people to Aerith.

She arched a brow. "I did not expect Queen Elara."

"I took this form to learn about your lives," I said. "There's no reason for me to be in my goddess form all the time."

Her eyebrow lowered. "From what I'd heard, you were lost in this form for a long time, your parents killed."

I nodded.

"How can a goddess have parents?" an Unseelie behind me asked.

"Where do you think this body came from?" I asked, turning to face the crowd. "I did not create it. I just put my soul into it when it was born. My consorts were put into their bodies as well."

"That must have been rough," Aerith said.

"Worse for some of us," Ryul whispered.

"Where are we to sit?" I asked. I didn't want to answer anymore questions.

Aerith waved at a table just to the left of hers that had food on it, but no one sitting at it. "That table has been set up for you."

I sat at the table, and my consorts put food on a plate, and then set it before me.

I started eating, and they made their plates to eat as well.

The room was full of quiet murmurs, but I didn't try to listen in on any of them. I just wanted to eat and then leave for the next continent.

"You're missing a consort, are you not?" Aerith asked from her place.

I almost choked on my food. I took a long drink of water before answering.

"Yes, we're leaving in the morning to go get him," I said.

"You know where he is?" she asked. The way she said it, she sounded smug.

"Of course, I do," I said. "I have a bond with them."

"That's what the mark on your neck is, isn't it, Myrin?" Aerith asked.

Myrin nodded. "It is, but we also have a metaphysical bond that the mark is not necessary for."

"How interesting," she whispered.

"You have one Unseelie and five Seelie," an Unseelie near the back said. "Why is that?"

"I did not choose which body my consorts would take. I do know that Myrin was the first Unseelie, so it makes sense for him to become Unseelie again," I said.

"The first Unseelie?" Aerith asked, eyes wide.

Myrin smirked. "Yes. I am the first."

The crowd gossiped loudly, and Myrin looked incredibly smug.

I finished eating and stood. "Thank you, Queen Aerith, for your hospitality. I will return and pick up those who are willing to return with me to the mainland."

"We will look forward to your return," she said, stood, and bowed to me.

We left the castle and were escorted by some guards to the docks.

I sat against the center mast and closed my eyes.

"You look exhausted," Ryul whispered.

I nodded.

"Is it because you're not with your last mate?" he asked.

"That's a big part," I said.

"Let's set out," Myrin said.

Ryul dropped a kiss on my head and went to help the others set sail.

I dozed on and off as we sailed away from the island.

Sometime during the night, the wind picked up, and the guys started yelling orders to each other.

The ship rocked wildly, and I slid across the deck.

I screeched, opening my eyes, and reaching for anything to grab as I slid towards the side of the ship.

Venali grabbed my forearm, jerking me to a stop. "Got you," he said.

I gripped his arm and smiled wide. "Hi."

He chuckled and pulled me up as he stood. "Napping on the deck isn't a good idea."

"I see that," I said. I held onto his side, hooking two of my fingers through his beltloop.

"Bring her up here," Myrin said.

Venali picked me up and carried me to Myrin and the ship's steering wheel.

I kissed Venali's cheek and then his lips when he turned his head. "Thank you."

"You're welcome." He set me down next to Myrin.

Myrin took a rope from his pack, tied it around my waist, and then tied me to the railing in front of the wheel. "This way, I can see you and I know you won't go flying off the ship," he said.

I glared at him, but decided it wasn't a terrible idea, so I let it happen.

For the first time, I looked out at the sea, and my mouth dropped open. The waves roiled and rose around us, some more than twice as high as the ship.

"We're going to die," I whispered.

"It's just a small storm," Myrin said. Then, the bastard laughed.

Lightning flashed and thunder boomed.

Amrynn dragged Ryul to stand beside me. "Stay with our queen," Amrynn ordered.

Ryul nodded and gripped the railing beside me with white knuckled intensity. His eyes were wide and full of terror as he watched the sea.

"Don't worry, Ryul. I've sailed in weather like this several times," Myrin said.

"Not reassuring," Ryul mumbled.

"What's wrong?" I asked Ryul.

"I can't swim," he whispered.

Oh, right. I'd forgotten.

I laid my hand on top of one of his and squeezed. "We'll be okay."

He wrapped his arm inside the ropes securing me to the railing, which helped me feel more secure as well.

The ship rocked to and fro, but the initial fear I had was gone now that I needed to reassure Ryul.

I set my hand on Ryul's atop the railing, and leaned my shoulder against his. It was cold, and my body trembled, but I tried to still as much as possible, not wanting him to think I shook from fear.

Myrin yelled orders to the others, and they ran about the ship, pulling ropes, and doing other things I had no idea about.

Hours passed, or what seemed like hours, and then the sea quieted and the sun came out from behind the clouds.

The waters stilled, and the ship sat in placid water.

Myrin sagged against the wheel and let out a tired groan.

Ryul quickly left, almost jerking away from me in his haste to be somewhere else.

I didn't let it bother me, though. Men like him didn't enjoy showing weakness.

After untying myself, I walked to Myrin and kissed his cheek. "You did well, Myrin."

He smiled, the movement slow and sleepy. "Thank you."

"Come on, let's get you to bed. I need you at full-strength should another storm show up," I said, and looped an arm around his waist and tugged his around my shoulders.

He picked me up, making me gasp, and carried me to the captain's cabin. "I'm not that tired, Elara."

"I am and I just stood there all night," I said and yawned.

He chuckled, shut the door behind us, and fell onto the bed with me on top of him.

I rolled off him, onto my side, and lay my head on his chest. "Storms have always interested me, but being in the middle of an ocean when there's one is not something I want to deal with again."

"We still have a long way to go," he mumbled.

"Go to sleep," I said. I jerked the blanket out from behind me, and tossed it over the both of us.

His snoring was almost immediate.

CHAPTER 26
RYUL

Fear was not something I was used to. Then again, being cooped up in a castle most of my life didn't leave room for much fear to enter.

My parents had tried to teach me to swim when I was a child, but I'd refused, saying there was no reason and I'd never need to swim.

Now, I wished I had listened.

As an adult, I hadn't been able to bring myself to ask anyone to teach me to swim.

Being in that storm, with nothing but water surrounding us, I had wished more than anything that I'd been taught to swim.

"You alright?" Durlan asked, setting a hand on my shoulder.

We all sat in the lower deck of the ship, around tables we'd rigged for eating our meals.

Elara and Myrin slept in the captain's quarters, Myrin's snores audible even down here.

I still didn't like him, but I respected him a bit more after watching how he captained the ship in the storm.

"Fine," I mumbled.

Amrynn sat across from me, a plate of food in each hand. He slid one towards me. "It's alright to be scared. Being scared once in a while is a good thing."

"I was scared at several points last night," Kydrus said. "Most notably when Elara started sliding down the deck."

That had terrified me. I'd wanted to grab her, but the fear of both of us falling into the water, with me unable to save her if that happened, had rooted me in place.

"I need you to teach me to swim," I said without looking at anyone of them in particular. At this point, I didn't care who it was, as long as it wasn't Myrin.

I shoveled food into my mouth, exhausted from my muscles being clenched so tight during the storm.

"When we get to land, we'll make some time for one of us to teach you," Durlan said.

I nodded.

"How can Elara sleep with Myrin snoring so loudly?" Venali asked and plopped down beside me at the table.

"She can't," Elara said, walking to join us.

She sat between Amrynn and Kydrus, leaning her head against Kydrus's shoulder.

The jealousy that had accompanied seeing her touching the others was gone now. With my memories back, I'd fully accepted my brothers being hers as well.

"Would you like to take a nap?" Kydrus asked.

She yawned, but shook her head. "No, I'll just sit here while you guys eat and maybe close my eyes."

All of us smirked.

She was a minute or less from falling asleep, and we all knew it.

Amrynn looped an arm around her waist, ensuring she wouldn't fall should the ship move suddenly while she napped.

"How many battles have you been in?" I asked Venali.

He smiled, but then frowned. "Too many to keep count, sadly."

"You?" I asked, turning and looking at Durlan.

"A dozen or so," he said.

"You've never been in one, have you?" Amrynn asked me.

I shook my head. "I stayed in the castle, protecting it from bandits."

"You regret that?" Kydrus asked.

I sighed and set my fork down. "I don't regret that I kept my word to Elara, to wait for her. I don't regret keeping the castle safe. But I do regret not learning more outside of books. I didn't understand how green I was until we went to the Unseelie. The situation was one I had no idea how to handle. And while I don't doubt my fighting abilities, I truly don't know what would happen if we were to fight in a large battle."

"Don't be too upset about not having to fight," Amrynn said. "Many of us wish we hadn't been in many of the battles we have. Yes, it gave us experience, but it also gave us nightmares, complexes, and we lost a lot of friends."

"Fighting isn't for everyone," Venali said. "It is important that you learn to defend yourself and our queen, but you don't have to experience battle to be ready for that."

Coming from Venali, that seemed like good advice. The brute loved battles.

"What is the plan when we reach this new continent?" I asked. Elara had kept close-lipped about it, so I had no idea what to expect.

"We aren't sure. We know she's going to find her final mate, and she wants to try to unite the continents, but we have no idea how," Durlan said. He scowled, and stabbed at his food.

He loved plans, and it seemed not having a plan bothered him a lot.

I agreed with him on that. Having plans made things so much easier.

"She needs to practice using her powers," I said. "Or she won't be able to prove she's really Amara."

"Have any of you felt *different* since you got your full memories back?" Amrynn asked.

We all nodded.

"I feel like I have another mode or set of powers I could be using," Kydrus said.

I nodded again. "Like she does when she turns into Amara. Like a god mode, right?"

Everyone nodded.

"But I haven't figured out how to unlock it," Amrynn said. "I tried right after Elara accepted herself, but despite feeling the powers and knowing they're there, I can't unlock them."

"Perhaps we have to wait until the final consort is here," Durlan said. "We aren't a complete unit yet. It could have something to do with that."

"Or, there's another barrier, something else she's holding back that we don't know about," Venali said, looking at Elara.

We all turned to look at her, peacefully sleeping on Kydrus's shoulder.

That was a possibility. She liked keeping secrets. And she hadn't figured out everything yet. Maybe we wouldn't be able to unlock our powers until she fully unlocked her ability to take her goddess form.

"She's awfully cute for such a damn handful," Venali whispered.

Durlan and I chuckled.

"You think we have the possibility of being reincarnated again?" I asked.

Durlan scowled and shook his head. "I don't think so. I think what happened last time was Amara's doing, but I am uncertain if she could do it again. Or, if she would want to do it again. If she can unite the continents, then there is no need for us to be reincarnated."

"I'd rather not go another thousand or so years without my mate again," Myrin said.

He sat on the other side of Durlan, looking spry and happy.

"Good nap?" I asked.

He nodded. His eyes fell to Elara. "My snoring kept her awake?" he asked.

We all nodded.

"Like it always did," Durlan said. "Even when she was a goddess, she couldn't handle your snoring."

"It's not like I can control it," Myrin said. He got up and grabbed some food from the crates.

"You'd think a goddess could fix something as simple as that," Kydrus said. His voice was soft, and not as deep as usual.

Was it to try to keep from waking Elara?

"She finds it endearing and doesn't want to fix it," Myrin said. "Or at least that is what she told me last lifetime."

"I think she just didn't want you to feel bad," I said, smirking.

Myrin chuckled and sat back down. "You might be right, brother. You might be right."

Part of me wanted to dislike him, distrust him still, but this new Myrin was improved. And, I was better this time. Or, I was trying to be at least. It was clear now that Myrin had no intention of harming Elara or Amara. And that his heart was exactly where mine was. To protect and love her for as long as we lived.

CHAPTER 27
ELARA

THE MOMENT LAND came into view, the connection with my last mate went taut and took my breath away for a moment.

Close. We were so close to him.

When we finally reached shore, I leapt from the ship and lay on the beach.

"Land!" I yelled, rolling on the warm sand. "We made it to Emortalia, finally."

The guys had to properly dock the boat, so they didn't join me for at least ten minutes.

Ryul was the first one to leave the ship, and he joined me, lying on the beach. "Land!"

I sat up and looked around, surprised that there were no other people around.

"I think we came to a port that's no longer used," Durlan said. "The ropes and everything are old."

"Should we sail elsewhere?" Venali asked.

"No," I snapped.

All eyes turned to me.

"He's close," I said, feeling my cheeks heat.

"Lead the way," Kydrus said and waved his arm inland.

I opened my bond and immediately felt a tug from the other end.

I turned slowly to the right until I faced the correct direction and then started walking.

Venali walked at my side, his hand on the sword at his hip.

"Excited?" he asked.

I glanced up at his face, finding him smiling at me. "Nervous," I said.

He frowned. "Why?"

"I don't know whether he's mad or not," I whispered.

"I'm sure he's not going to be mad at you," Myrin said behind me.

"It's not your fault he ended up on a different continent," Kydrus said.

"He may not know that," I said. "Just like Ryul didn't know that I had forgotten my memories and been taken as a slave."

All of them growled, which made me smirk.

"Well, even if he is mad, when we first see him, he will quickly get over it and forgive you," Venali said.

"I hope so," I whispered.

The sand was hard to walk up, and my progress was slow.

We finally made it out of the sand, and I released a happy sigh. "Let's not live near sand," I said.

Several chuckles followed my statement.

The bond tugged me to the left, so I altered our course towards it.

"You sure you know where you're going?" Amrynn asked.

I turned around to glare at him, walking backwards, opened my mouth to give a snappy retort, and tripped. My arms windmilling as I tried to keep from falling.

Venali grabbed my arm and pulled, helping me regain my balance.

"Thanks," I said, turned around, and resumed walking.

"I don't think I've seen her so flustered since before she remembered she was a royal," Kydrus commented.

We entered a heavily wooded area, and I had to dodge and weave around trees as we climbed up a hill. The connection felt stronger, and it felt like he was coming towards us.

"I think he's trying to find us, too," I said, picking up my speed.

We crested the hill. On this side, there were trees, but they weren't as dense, and there were several open areas, giving me a clear view.

And there, at the bottom was a man with golden hair, flowing in the wind. He raised his head, and our gazes locked.

Him.

Mate.

Mine.

His physical appearance was different, but there was no doubt who he was. The bond between us was undeniable.

Before I realized what I was doing, I ran down the hill, sliding and grabbing trees to keep my descent at a reasonable pace.

The others called out to me, but I paid them no mind. I had to get to him. I had to touch him.

He ran up the mountain towards me, his eyes glowing a soft amber, and his lips pulled up in a beautiful smile.

My hands were covered in sap and leaves, and the next time I tried to grab a tree, my grip slipped.

I yelped and started to fall, but warm, muscular arms wrapped around me, pulling me to a stop, and against an even warmer body.

"You," he whispered, "are just as crazy as the last lifetime, it seems."

"You're here. I'm here. We're here," I gasped out.

Lifting my head, I fell into his gaze and wasn't sure I wanted to ever be pulled out.

"My goddess, what are you doing in this body?" he asked and stroked my cheek.

"The same thing you are," I whispered, licking my lips.

He watched the movement like a starved wolf following prey.

"Are you mad?" I asked.

He arched a brow. "Mad?"

Loud crashing behind us drew his attention, though his eyes did not leave mine he tilted his head that direction.

"Brothers," he said without looking away from me.

"She's worried you're mad at her for putting us in these forms, and for being separated," Myrin said. "Though, she didn't choose our forms."

"I'm not mad. I've been dying to find you since you connected the bond, though," he said.

He had a strong jaw with light stubble. It was rather sexy. I wondered if I should have been bothered that he was human, but he didn't seem like a normal human.

"What are you?" Ryul asked.

"He looks human," Amrynn said.

"A shifter," my mate said. "I'll explain all about me later. First, I have something I need to do."

My brows furrowed and anger began to build within me. What could he have to do that was more important than me? I was his mate, separated for far too long, and he had more important things to do?

He tucked some hair behind my ear, smirked, and whispered into the now uncovered ear, "You may be in a different body, but your expressions are the same. You misunderstood what I meant."

"What did you mean then?" I asked.

He gripped my waist, pulled back enough to look into my eyes, and said, "That I needed to do this." His mouth crashed into mine, and he kissed me with a ferocity I felt equally.

I wrapped my arms around his neck and kissed him deeply.

Our bond solidified, and I gasped, pulling back from the kiss.

He smiled down at me and said, "That was much more important than showing them what a shifter is."

CHAPTER 28
ELARA

"What name do you go by?" I asked.

"Daniel," my golden-haired consort said.

"I go by Elara," I said. "In this form at least."

"Let's talk about these forms," he said and folded his arms across his chest.

He had biceps as large as Venali's. And a chest as wide.

"My eyes are up here," Daniel said, but I could hear the teasing in his tone.

"I wanted to experience life as my people do, so I could better understand their hardships," I said.

"Was this the plan should we die all along?" he asked.

I nodded.

"Did you know we were going to die?" he asked.

I shook my head. "I was concerned we might, but I don't see the future, never could."

"What is a shifter?" Durlan asked.

"It's a man who transforms into an animal," I answered, talking before Daniel could.

Daniel smiled. "How did you know that?"

"I read a book about Minloa history. It mentioned shifters," I said.

"You can transform into an animal? Like, any animal or a specific one?" Amrynn asked.

"A specific animal," Daniel said. His body glowed, and then before me stood a large golden-brown bear.

My hands and face were in his fur within seconds. "So warm," I whispered, rubbing my face in the thick and shaggy fur.

"That's intimidating," Venali said.

Daniel shifted back, which caused me to be cuddled up against his chest while he was squatted down. He picked me up, and I burrowed my face into his neck.

"I'll take you to my house," Daniel said. "Expect stares. People haven't seen Seelie or Unseelie in a very long time here."

"I can walk," I whispered.

"Nope," Daniel said. "I'm not letting you go the rest of the day. Maybe the rest of the week."

I was okay with that.

"She looks very disappointed," Amrynn said and laughed.

"We might have to pry them apart so she can do what she came here to do," Kydrus said.

"I'll tear your arms off if you try to separate us," Daniel said. The growl in his throat was deep, much deeper than a Seelie growl.

"Your growl is different than ours," I whispered to him.

He glanced down at me. "Well, I am an animal. Does it bother you?"

I shook my head and then rested it on his shoulder. "No, just commenting on it. I like it, actually."

"She says that until she has to hear him growling for an hour while we catch him up on what's happened," Myrin muttered.

"What's happened?" Daniel asked, slowing so he could walk beside Myrin.

"No," I snapped. "No serious talk until after I get some time with Daniel."

Myrin raised his hands in surrender. "As the queen wishes."

"Queen?" Daniel asked.

"Queen of the Seelie," Durlan said.

"Well, that's interesting," Daniel whispered. "I thought goddess was better, but queen does open other doors for you while in this form."

"How far is your house?" I asked.

I ran my fingertips over the stubble on his chin, loving the roughness. Seelie and Unseelie did not grow facial hair.

"Not far," Daniel said. He glanced down at me. "You seem fascinated by my hair."

"We don't grow beards," Myrin said. "You're the only of us who does."

Daniel smirked and for a moment I stopped breathing as I took him in. My other consorts were handsome, but Daniel was glorious. He oozed masculinity, even more than Venali.

"Stop drooling," Ryul grumbled.

Daniel licked the corners of my lips. "No evidence."

Sense left me, I grabbed his face, tilted it to the side, and kissed him, thrusting my tongue into his mouth and refusing to let him turn his head at all.

He kissed me back, his hands tightening on my body where he held me.

I pulled back, panting, and hid my face against his neck, closing my eyes. "Sorry."

"Don't apologize," he said, his voice rough. He cleared his throat. "I wasn't trying to tease you."

Exiting the forest, we entered a small village. Humans walked around, and many openly stared at us.

"Humans," I whispered and swallowed hard.

Amrynn stepped closer to me, his hand reaching out to rest on my forearm. "It's not the same ones," he whispered.

"What's wrong?" Daniel asked, looking from me to Amrynn.

"It's all part of our story," Amrynn said. "Lots to tell you."

"I didn't know we had humans on our world," I whispered.

"They're pretty harmless," Daniel said, but his hold on me tightened when he felt me shaking.

Amrynn and I growled at the same time.

"Okay," Daniel said, drawing the word out. He walked to a house along the outer edge of the village and pushed open the door. The guys walked in, and then Daniel walked past them, down a long hallway, and to a huge bedroom with a giant bed in it. He kicked the door shut behind him, slid his boots off, and set me on the edge of the bed. My legs hung over the edge, and he spread them so he could stand between my legs, and in front of me.

"While I would love to make love to you right now, I think we need to talk first," he whispered.

"They can help tell you what's happened better," I said, swallowing thickly.

Humans. Why did it have to be humans?

"You slept with men before them," he whispered. "Why?"

My head jerked up, and my mouth dropped. "I, uh, it isn't what you think. I didn't cheat on you. I didn't have my memories. I didn't know I was Amara until a couple months ago. If you let them explain, you'll understand."

"Who were these other men?" he asked.

How did he even know?

"They were no one. Just sex. Not even good sex. I didn't know. I didn't remember you. If I had, I wouldn't have slept with them. I swear." The words tumbled out of my mouth quickly, and tears began to build.

He exhaled and met my eyes. "Okay. I believe you."

"You said you didn't remember until the bond was formed with the others," I said. "So, you didn't—"

He shook his head. "I didn't."

"Most of them did," I said. "I can't fault them because they didn't know."

"I forgive you, Amara. It still hurts, but I can't hold it against you if you didn't have your memory."

The others hadn't made a big deal out of it. They were jealous, but hadn't been upset. I wasn't sure what to do.

Daniel wiped his thumb across my cheek, wiping away a few stray tears. "Come on, let's go talk to the others. I need to know what's happened to you."

I tried to slide off the bed, but he picked me up again. I frowned. "I can walk. You don't have to touch me if you don't want to."

"Amara, I—"

"Elara," I corrected. "I'm Elara in this form."

His brows furrowed, but he said, "Elara, I didn't mean to upset you. I just needed to know. I can smell them on you."

"That was over a decade ago," I said. "How can you still smell them?"

He said, "My nose is very sensitive. And when you share your body with another person, it leaves a mark."

"I'm sorry, Daniel. I—" I didn't know what else to say. I felt like I should beg him for forgiveness, but at the same time, it wasn't fair that he was putting this on me since I hadn't had my memory.

He walked to the living room where the others sat on the couches, talking quietly.

All eyes turned to me when we entered.

"Why is she crying?" Kydrus asked, his lip pulling up in a snarl.

"I smelled her previous sexual partners. I asked her about it," Daniel said.

"You can't fault her for that. She didn't remember even this form's life," Amrynn said.

Daniel sat, positioning me in his lap. "Tell me what's happened."

I stood off his lap and sat on Myrin's instead, burying my face against his chest.

Myrin rubbed my back and kissed the top of my head.

"She was born the daughter of the king and queen of the Seelie of Minloa," Durlan began.

It took an hour, all of them adding bits and pieces, but they finally finished the story of my life so far.

Daniel had sat quietly the whole time, not moving, growling, or making any noise.

"That's it," Durlan said.

"So far," Kydrus said and chuckled.

"Myrin, you and I need to talk later," Daniel said.

Myrin nodded. "Okay."

"My goddess," Daniel whispered.

I turned my head so I could see him, but looked at him from beneath my hair, using it as a veil between us. "Yes?"

"Come here, please?" he requested.

"No," I said.

His brows furrowed. "No?"

I stood, the anger that had been growing finally surged to the top. "No. I haven't reacted that way since Amrynn on that damn spaceship. I'm not that pathetic girl. I can't believe I let you make me feel that way. So, no. I'm not going to come to you. If you want to talk to me, you can wait. You can wait until I'm done being mad. Maybe you can wait a bit longer, too."

"Elara," Myrin whispered.

I spun and exited the room, searched until I found a back door, and then walked out into the forest.

"Elara," Ryul called.

"Leave me," I ordered him. "I don't want to see any of you for a bit. I just need some time."

"Did you stop to consider that you might be mad because you're mad at yourself for not remembering who you are sooner?" Ryul asked. "That you aren't really mad at Daniel?"

"You say one more word, and I'll take your voice," I threatened him, spinning around to glare at him. "I'm tired of you guys treating me like a broken doll. I can protect myself. I can be mad if I want to. I have feelings. I'm allowed to have them."

Ryul sighed. "I didn't say you weren't allowed to have

feelings, I'm just—"

"Ryul! Leave me alone!" Power whipped around me, causing my hair and the leaves to float.

Ryul glared at me, but turned and left me alone.

I walked deeper into the forest. Humans. I had to deal with humans. Convincing them to unite with us might be more difficult than I thought.

Yes, I was mad at myself. But I was also mad at Daniel. If he'd just let us explain my past first, this could have been avoided. This unease inside of me would not be there.

I sat against a tree, leaning my head back and closing my eyes. Queen. Goddess. Slave. Seelie. They all fit me. Yet, I didn't feel like I fit any of them at the same time.

Did it count as cheating since I hadn't remembered them?

I knew the others had slept with women, and I hadn't been angry with them. Wasn't angry with them.

"I've upset you," Daniel whispered.

My eyes opened, and I stared at him crouched before me. He'd moved so silently. Was that part of being a shifter?

"Yes," I said.

"I should have let them tell me first. I shouldn't have isolated you to accuse you like that. I'm sorry. This was not how I wanted our reunion to go."

I stood and turned away from him. "Me neither, but here we are."

"You endured a lot. I only added to that. I'm a jerk."

"Yep." I headed deeper into the forest, farther away from his house.

"Elara," he called.

"Leave me alone to cool off," I said. "I just need space."

CHAPTER 29
MYRIN

Ryul stomped into the house, muttering to himself about stubborn women. Clearly, he was talking about our goddess.

"Didn't go like you planned?" I asked with a smirk.

He cut me a glare. "He's stalking her. Maybe he'll be able to calm her down."

"Or, she might just need some time to herself," I said and shrugged. "We've been at her side non-stop for a month. Everyone needs some alone time every now and then."

"Why's she so mad?" Ryul asked. "I told her she's really just mad at herself, which only made her madder."

Kydrus, Amrynn, Venali, Durlan, and I looked at each other, and then at him.

"You can't be that stupid," I said.

His fists clenched at his sides. "What?"

"Why would you say something so stupid to her?" Amrynn asked.

"What are you talking about? It's the truth," Ryul said.

"That's beside the point. Do you want her pointing out the stupid shit you did before and when you get mad, just remind you that you did it so you can only be mad at yourself? You'd still be upset with her, right?" Kydrus asked.

"She's mad at him. Yes, she's a little mad at herself, but right now she is mad at him. He accused her of cheating on him. She got upset because technically she did cheat on us, but she didn't remember. We cheated on her, too," Durlan said. "We didn't beg her for forgiveness. We didn't feel bad. Why? Because we recognized that it was before our memories were back. If we could go back in time and not do that, we would."

"There's a lot I would change if I could go back in time," I murmured.

"She's going to give you the cold shoulder again," Amrynn said and folded his arms across his chest. "I feel like I should punch you in the face, just because you deserve it."

"Same," Venali growled.

Ryul stared at us. "You're telling me I shouldn't point out her problems?"

"We're telling you that she's aware of the problems. When she's upset is not the time to pile them onto her," I said.

Ryul threw up his hands and walked out of the house.

Durlan looked at me. "Are you going to go after her?"

I shook my head. "Let's leave Daniel and her alone for a bit. The bear can protect her."

Durlan nodded and relaxed back against the couch.

Venali glared at the door Ryul left through. "That boy needs an attitude adjustment."

"He's young," I said. "He was young last lifetime. He'll learn."

"Before or after he hurts her more?" Amrynn asked.

I couldn't respond to that because that was exactly what I was worried about.

CHAPTER 30

ELARA

DANIEL WAS FOLLOWING ME. I could sense him, even if I couldn't hear him.

Why was it so hard for them to leave me alone? I was capable of protecting myself.

"Can't you just leave me alone?" I growled.

"Please, let me apologize properly," Daniel said.

I growled, clenched my fists, and spun around to face him. "Fine."

He stepped out from behind some trees to my right, nearly scaring me out of my skin.

He dropped to one knee and bowed his head. "I'm sorry. I'm a jerk. I messed up. I've been dying to find you and instead of focusing on the joy of being united, I overreacted and didn't give you a true chance to explain all that has happened. Please, forgive me, and let us go back to the beginning. Please?"

"I can't forget it happened," I whispered. No, that thought was now lodged in my brain. "But I can give you a chance to make it up to me."

He lifted his head. "Anything."

"Follow me," I ordered.

He obeyed, following right on my heels as I led him back to the house. I took him into the bedroom and spun around.

He shut the door to his room, and faced me, his eyes uncertain.

"I want to solidify our bond," I said.

He stripped his clothes off in seconds and then looked down at me.

I undressed slowly, well aware of his eyes on me the whole time.

He licked his lips.

"Are you going to be okay touching me when you can smell the others on me?" I asked. I hated that I sounded unsure, emotional, about it. I sounded like a self-conscious woman, which really irked me.

He wrapped me up in his arms, our bare skin touching, and his like an inferno against mine. "Yes. I will smother you in my scent, so it won't ever be brought up again."

I chuckled and rubbed my face against his chest. "I like the sound of that."

He picked me up and set me on the bed. Then he kissed me deeply. "You're so beautiful. So perfect." He kissed his way down my throat, to my breasts, and all the way down until he licked the spot that ached with need.

"Yes," I gasped and threw my head back.

With the skill of his tongue, I orgasmed faster than I ever had before. He licked his lips, and climbed up until he was positioned over me. He pressed his erection against my opening and stared down into my eyes. "You're the most perfect woman who has ever existed," he said. "I will worship you for the rest of our lives and beyond, through all of eternity." He slid inside of me slowly, closing his eyes and moaning when he was fully sheathed.

I moaned as well, the feel of him inside of me, finally, was orgasmic on its own.

His hips began moving, and I gripped his back, trying not to dig my nails into him.

He kissed my breasts and then sucked on one of my nipples as he continued his steady rhythm.

Our bond pulled tight, and when we shared our orgasm, it fully solidified.

We lay together, breathing heavily, and a smile on both of our faces.

Instead of dressing after cleaning up, we lay back down and took a nap.

Sometime later, Myrin woke me. "You need to eat, Elara. We can hear your stomach in the front room."

I stretched and squealed. Why did stretching feel so good?

Two pairs of hungry eyes stared at me.

"Food," I reminded Myrin.

He held out my clothes. "Dress first."

I sat up, leaning on my hands behind me, and giving them an unblocked view of my bare breasts. "Maybe I don't want to get dressed."

"Maybe I would rather make a meal of you," Myrin said.

I smiled and grabbed my clothes. "Food first."

Myrin tossed Daniel a pair of pants. "You, too."

Daniel chuckled. "Fine. I'll put pants on."

Someone knocked on the front door, and we all tensed.

Daniel finished slipping into his pants and walked down the hallway to a answer it. "Yes?" he asked the visitor.

"Can I borrow a cup of sugar?" a silky female voice asked.

My hackles instantly went up.

"One second," Daniel said. He left the door open, which gave the woman a perfect line of sight to the bedroom, and to me sitting naked on Daniel's bed.

Her cheeks flushed, and she dropped her eyes.

Daniel brought her a bag of sugar and held it out.

"I didn't realize you associated with Seelie," she said.

"They just arrived," Daniel said.

"Didn't waste time," she muttered.

"No, I didn't waste time bedding my mate," Daniel said, his tone harsh.

The woman's head jerked up, her eyes wide. "Mate? She's your mate?"

Daniel nodded.

The woman gave me a once over.

I kept my relaxed posture, meeting her stare with one of my own.

"Thanks for the sugar," she said and spun around.

Daniel shut the door and growled something too soft for me to make out.

"Someone has an admirer." I dressed to avoid looking at him or Myrin.

"You don't know the half of it," Daniel muttered. "Even telling her you're my mate won't stop her from trying."

Death would stop her.

"No killing," Myrin said.

I mocked him silently.

Once dressed, I walked out of the room and to the

kitchen. Everyone else was already there, helping to make our meal.

"Her jealousy is so sexy, isn't it?" Venali asked Daniel.

Daniel smartly kept his mouth closed, though I did see his lips twitch.

"Tomorrow, I need you to take me to the leaders of Emortalia," I said.

"Are you going to be okay addressing humans?" Amrynn asked.

"Yes. I understand that these are not the same humans as the last," I said, slightly miffed that he asked me that, but at the same time I did understand.

"Are you going to go all goddess on them?" Ryul asked.

I didn't look at him, his comments from earlier were still upsetting. "I'm not going to reveal I am a goddess to anyone else. I will use my powers to persuade them to name me Empress, and fall into an alliance with Minloa. They can keep their rulers as is, but I will oversee everything."

"Why didn't you do the same with the Unseelie?" Myrin asked.

My cheek twitched. "Because she overstepped her boundaries."

"Because you lost your temper," Myrin said.

I growled, but couldn't refute his statement.

"They're likely to fight back," Daniel said.

I sighed. "Children always resist their parents. In the end, they'll see the light."

All of my consorts turned and looked at me with wide eyes.

"What?" I asked.

"Your personalities are blending more," Myrin said. "That's something Amara said before."

I shrugged. "It was bound to happen eventually. We are the same person."

"After food, you need to practice your magic," Durlan said.

I nodded. I'd already planned to work on the longevity of holding my goddess form.

The guys shared a look and then went back to making our meal.

"I'm going to go practice now," I said and stood. "Using my magic will make me hungry."

Durlan nodded. "Good point."

"I'll go with you," Daniel said.

Ryul opened his mouth to say something, but Venali elbowed him.

Daniel followed me to the living room.

I sat in the center of the floor and crossed my legs. "You can sit over there," I said and pointed at the couch.

He sat on the couch and watched silently.

Closing my eyes, I let everything fall away except for the magic in my core. With a slight tug, the powers released, and I took on my goddess form. Something felt different, my consciousness as Elara was dripping away until I was only Amara.

Daniel straightened as our connection sizzled between us. "Amara," he whispered.

I turned and smiled.

He slid off the couch and knelt before me.

With one hand, I pushed back his hair and kissed his cheek. "A bear is a rather fitting animal for you," I said.

"Your voice is different," he whispered.

"I have Amara's voice when I'm Amara and Elara's voice when I'm Elara," I said. "We aren't fully merged, and I'm not sure if we will ever fully merge. It will take you time to get used to the difference, but we have a lot of time left together."

He wrapped his arms around me and kissed my ear. "I've missed you, my goddess."

"I've missed you as well, my consort."

"How long can you hold this body without negatively affecting the fae body you're inhabiting?" he asked.

"Not very long, unfortunately, but her strength is improving. Soon, I should be able to come and go as necessary," I said.

"Go? Why would you need to go?" he asked, pulling back to look down into my eyes.

"This world needs Elara. She is a symbol of hope and peace. I am a goddess, yes, but the people need someone who has been through the trials and tribulations that she has," I said.

Something dark touched the corner of my mind.

I pushed Daniel away, stood, and turned towards it. I'd felt this darkness before. I *knew* this darkness.

It drew closer, curious, but hesitant.

My body shuddered and before I wanted to, I had to release the powers.

I collapsed onto the floor, gasping for breath. Fully Elara again.

"What happened?" Durlan asked as he rushed to my side.

"What was that feeling?" Ryul asked.

"Evil," Myrin said. "That was what evil feels like."

"Not evil really," I gasped. "Just...darkness."

"What was it?" Daniel asked. "I've never felt anything like it before."

"You have, you just don't remember," Myrin said. He squatted down beside my head and rested his hand on my cheek. "It was him, wasn't it?"

"I don't know," I whispered. "I had to release my powers before I could figure out what it was."

"What are you talking about?" Amrynn asked Myrin.

"Do you remember how we died?" Myrin asked.

"I do," Kydrus said softly, his eyes haunted.

"No, we don't," Durlan said.

"We were killed by a god," Myrin said and stood. "In the universe there must be balance. Good and evil. Light and dark. Amara is the light. The good. He is the dark. The evil."

"What's his name?" Ryul asked.

I slapped my hand over Myrin's mouth out of instinct. My cheeks heated as he looked at me. "I don't think we should say or even think the name."

He moved my hand away and nodded. "I agree."

My vision began to swim, and I slumped into Durlan. "Dizzy," I whispered.

Durlan began to heal me, to give me some of his power, but I pushed away. "No, let me be. I need to get used to this fatigue. I need to work through this and figure out how to function even while it weighs heavily on my limbs."

"Well, you're awake this time, which is an improvement," Ryul said.

I laughed. "True."

Carefully, I pushed myself up to my feet, swaying slightly.

Several pairs of hands reached out towards me, but I held my hands out and they all pulled away.

"See, I've got this," I said with a wide smile.

The guys looked unconvinced.

"I'm goo—"

Before I could finish my sentence, my eyes rolled up into the back of my head and I fainted.

CHAPTER 31
DANIEL

Venali, Ryul, and I caught Elara before she hit the floor.

My little goddess always liked to overextend herself.

"She's sleeping," Durlan said, waving his hand over her body to check her vitals.

I let Venali take her and lay her on the couch. Then I sat on the other end, so I could run my fingers through her hair.

"She hasn't changed," I said with a laugh.

"Nope," Myrin agreed. "She's still the same, reckless woman as before."

"What was she talking about?" Ryul asked. "The darkness?"

"You said we were killed by a god," I said to Myrin.

He sighed and ran a hand through his hair with a growl. "We were basically gods, once Amara took us as consorts. We weren't easily killed. How else do you think we would have died?"

"A god killed us. Why?" Ryul asked.

"Because he was jealous," Myrin said. "He wanted

Amara, but she told him she could not be his consort. He could not understand why she refused him. He was power-ful, the most powerful being in the universe, next to Amara. To prove his power, he started taking us out. Amara fought him, trying to save us. We caused her death in the end."

"You think he still wants her? That he will try to claim her for himself again?" I asked. Had I been in bear form, my claws would have dug into the arm of the couch. She was mine, ours, and we would not let some pompous god take her just because he was jealous.

"Most likely," Myrin said.

"Why didn't you tell us this before?" Ryul asked, snarling.

"I had hoped he was hibernating or had moved on. I hoped he would not bother us again. Amara proved that she would rather die than be with him. We'll have to be wary from now on," Myrin said.

"What did she mean about leaving? That this world needed Elara, but not her?" I asked. "She can't mean that she'll cease to exist, can she?" That thought sent a shiver of dread through me. It wouldn't be the first time that she came up with a crazy-ass plan.

No one responded, which was response enough.

What would that mean for us? What would that do to Elara to have Amara separated from her?

There were too many unknowns in our future that I did not like at all.

Elara sat up, looked around, and asked, "How long was I asleep?"

"Just a few minutes," Durlan said.

She smiled and lay back down. "I'm getting better."

"Yes, you are," I said and stroked her hair.

And, I would do everything in my power to keep her from dying this time. Even it if meant dying again myself.

CHAPTER 32
ELARA

THE HUMANS GATHERED WERE VERY unlike the ones Amrynn and I had met during our kidnapping. These ones were relatively docile and much more fearful.

Was it because they didn't have the advanced technology and knew I was more powerful as a Seelie?

Daniel had advised us that this continent, Emortalia, was broken up into three sections. Carnel, where humans and shapeshifters lived together. Plunce, where shapeshifters lived. And Distra, where humans lived. They were separated by the peoples' prejudices, but Daniel said it helped keep the peace to have a place for like-minded people to go. I thought it was stupid.

Daniel led us to a large building with a giant metal bell atop it. A few men were stationed out front, guards by the look of the swords on their hips. Daniel spoke to the guards for a moment, and then one went inside while the other gave me a glare.

"I don't think he likes me," I whispered to Myrin, who stood on my right.

Myrin snickered. "Or, he's wondering why I'm with you when you're Seelie and they know our kind hate each other."

"That will be fixed soon enough," I said.

The guard who'd left returned and waved us in.

I walked by the guard who was still glaring with my head held high.

I followed behind Daniel with Myrin at my back. The others had wanted to come, but I'd convinced them that bringing so many Seelie into one room would make the humans way too uncomfortable.

We were led to an open room with seating around the edges and a platform where three humans sat. The middle seat was the tallest, obviously meant to be a throne despite being made of wood, and had a fat, balding man sitting in it. Beside him was a woman in a pretty dress and his other side was a young adult boy.

Daniel stopped before the humans. "Greetings, Your Majesties. I bring before you Elara, Queen of the Seelie."

Several humans in the audience murmured to each other. The royals didn't even move.

"What can I do for you, Queen of the Seelie?" the king asked.

"I've come here on a mission of peace," I said, taking a step forward. "I've come to request that we unite our continents and kingdoms and foster better relations."

"Why should we unite with your kingdom?" the boy asked.

The king gave him a glare, but didn't say anything else, so I assumed they wanted me to answer.

"We have many things worth trading. We are powerful

and have healers who could heal your people better than medicine alone," I said.

"And what do you want from us?" the king asked.

"Peace and unity," I said.

"You wish to open trade with us and barter for becoming allies?" the queen asked.

I nodded. "Yes."

"I find this very suspect," the king said.

I smiled. "We can sign a written trade agreement to ensure there is no miscommunication about our partnership."

"Very well," the king said. "I will review the trade agreement and if it is to my liking, I will sign it."

I glanced at Myrin who stepped forward with the rolled-up agreement in his hand.

The guards stepped forward, their spears aimed at him.

Myrin held out the agreement. "For your review," he said.

One of the guards pulled back his spear, took the agreement, and then handed it to the king.

The king opened it, and we stood in silence while he read it. He took quite a long time, and I began to wonder if he couldn't read. Several moments later, he raised his head and looked at me. "You're naming yourself Empress?"

I smiled. "More like advising you of my title."

"You think you can rule over us?" he asked.

"I have no intention of disrupting your rule of Carnel or taking anything away from you," I said. "I'm simply advising you of my true title. I will be going to the other rulers of the other continent to obtain their alliance as well."

"What of your own fighting between the Seelie and Unseelie?" the queen asked.

"That has ended," I said and waved towards Myrin. "As you can see, one of my consorts is Unseelie."

"And they have united under you, the Empress of the Galaxy?" the king asked.

I smiled. "Yes."

"May I read the agreement?" the queen asked.

The king handed it to her, and we waited while she read it. She sighed and said, "There is nothing in here giving her any powers over us. It is just giving her a title. Let the Seelie Queen have her title and let us open up peaceful trade between our peoples. The plagues have been bad this summer, and I would rather our people be healed with their assistance than die by our hesitation."

I really liked this queen.

"You are a wise and beautiful queen," I said. "I am glad we are able to make this agreement."

"Do you have any healers with you?" the queen asked.

The king signed the agreement and then motioned at me to come forward to sign. I did and then stepped back.

"I do have a healer," I said. "Do you have many who are sick?"

"About a handful," she said.

I turned to Myrin. "Will that be too many for Durlan?"

He shook his head. "No, but even if it was, many of us can heal also."

"How many consorts do you have?" the king asked, an eyebrow arched.

"Seven," I said.

The queen's eyes widened.

"Where are your sick?" I asked. "I'll fetch my consort right away."

"I'll show you," she said and stood.

Two women with swords came around from behind the queen's chair. I hadn't seen them standing back there, and that impressed me more than I liked to admit.

"This way," she said and walked out of the room with her two female guards behind her.

"I like her," I whispered to Daniel.

Daniel smiled. "I thought you might."

"When we get back to Daniel's home, we are going to talk, Empress," Myrin whispered in my ear.

I chuckled and continued walking without responding.

The queen waited for us outside of the building, her guards eyeing Myrin with suspicion and, if I wasn't mistaken, lust.

The urge to snarl at them was almost uncontrollable.

"This way," the queen said.

I caught up to her and walked at her side, though several feet apart. "Your land is beautiful," I said. "Are there more than humans here?"

She smiled. "We have shifters, as I'm sure you're aware with Daniel at your side. We also have some humans with a bit of magic, but sadly none of their magic includes healing."

Humans with magic?

"What type of magic do these humans have?" I asked, my voice a little too high for my liking.

"They can conjure fire, move water, and other elemental things," Daniel said.

"Like a toddler fae?" Myrin asked.

Daniel nodded. "Yes, but they don't progress beyond that."

"Are there fae creatures here?" I asked the queen.

"I'm not sure what you consider fae creatures or just creatures," she said. She looked at Daniel. "Do you know?"

He nodded. "We have a few fae creatures, but none of the truly dangerous ones."

I exhaled. "Thank goodness." There were some seriously dangerous creatures that I couldn't imagine the humans being able to protect themselves from without magic.

The queen led us to a large building with a giant "T" on it. "What does the 'T' stand for?" I asked.

"That's a cross, a symbol of the god of healing," she said.

"God of healing? Who do you pray to?" I asked, trying to keep the disgust from my voice. They definitely weren't praying to me.

"The god of healing," the queen said with furrowed brows. "Surely you have heard of him."

"Perhaps if you told me his name?" I requested.

"Dakath," she said.

I stopped walking and stared up at the symbol. Dakath was the name Durlan had gone by in our last lifetime. They prayed to Durlan. The one I was going to bring to them to heal their people.

"Breathe," Myrin whispered in my ear.

"If I could bring Dakath here, would that seal my claim as Empress?" I asked the queen.

She spun around, her eyes wide. "You could bring him here? You speak to the gods?"

"If I could, would that seal my claim with you? Would you agree to refer to me as Empress?" I asked again.

"Yes," she said, her voice breathy.

I turned to Myrin. "Bring me my consort."

Myrin bowed and ran off, his stride so long that it took him out of the town before the queen had time to gasp.

I closed my eyes and acted like I was praying or summoning Durlan. I let a bit of my magic out, to let my body glow as I felt them approaching.

Several humans nearby gasped.

"She's glowing," one human woman said, though I wasn't sure who she was.

I opened my eyes and said, "Dakath, God of Healing, please assist these humans in their time of need."

The queen looked at me with uncertainty, and then Durlan teleported to stand beside me. "My Empress," he said and then bowed to me. "I am at your service."

"He's...it's him," the queen gasped.

"He bowed to her. He called her Empress," one of the queen's guards said to the queen.

Durlan straightened and faced the queen. "Show me to your sick so I may heal them."

She bowed to him and then quickly pushed open the doors and waved him in.

I started to follow, but Durlan turned to me and said, "Stay here, Empress. I will cure the sick and return to you, but I do not want their sickness to touch or taint you."

I dipped my head. "Very well."

Durlan shut the door behind him and Myrin jogged back to me. "You remembered that was his name after she said it, didn't you?" he asked.

I nodded. "I don't remember your names, but after she said it, it came to me. I remember our lives, events that happened, but not your names for some reason."

Myrin smiled. "Names are changeable and unimportant. Only the soul is what truly matters."

Daniel nudged me and guided me across the street to sit on the porch of a building there. We sat, watching the building that housed their sick. I couldn't tell what happened inside the building, but didn't really care. Depending on how sick the people were and how many there were, we could be there awhile.

"Thirsty?" Daniel asked.

I nodded. "And hungry."

"I'll get us food," he said and walked off.

Myrin sat beside me. "You look better today than you have since I found you."

"Probably since I used my powers recently," I said. I leaned back on my hands and watched the humans going about their lives.

Would they learn to make weapons like Barry's people did? Or something worse?

"You're scowling," Myrin whispered.

"The humans we encountered had advanced weaponry," I whispered. "I'm wondering if these humans will develop the same in their future."

"Humans are intelligent and inquisitive creatures by nature. They're also easily scared, and I don't doubt they'll come up with some type of creation to help protect themselves. Especially, since they'll be in contact with our kind more. We're terrifying to them," Myrin said.

"Is it our pointy teeth and ears?" I asked and bared my teeth at him.

He bared his teeth back at me.

Both of us laughed, and I leaned my shoulder against his.

I didn't have favorites amongst my guys, but my connection with Myrin was definitely the strongest. He was my first consort however many thousands of years ago we'd met, so I supposed it made sense.

A few female humans slowed as they passed us, their eyes firmly locked on Myrin. Their cheeks heated, and they hurried by.

I looked over at him and saw the smile he'd given them. "You're going to make the men jealous if you flirt with the humans like that."

"Not you?" he asked.

I rolled my eyes. "You're not going to leave me. Not after this long."

He leaned over and kissed my cheek. "Never," he whispered in my ear.

Daniel returned with a basket of food and three mugs of water held in one of his hands.

Myrin took the mugs from him and handed me one.

I guzzled from it, not realizing how thirsty I actually was.

Daniel sat on the porch beside me and removed the cloth that had been covering the food.

"What is this stuff?" I asked. "It smells good, but I've never seen many of these things."

"Just eat," he said and chuckled. "I promise it's all safe."

I picked up one of the purplish round items. It was soft like a fruit. I sniffed it. It smelled sweet, too. I took a bite and my eyes widened. The inside was very sweet, but the skin was a little bitter, which combined made it delicious.

I grabbed another item and tried it. It was yellow and inside and outside was bitter.

Daniel laughed at me. "Your face."

"You put that in there on purpose, didn't you?" I asked, putting the yellow thing back in the basket.

He shrugged while smirking.

We ate in silence, the humans giving us a wide berth, and waited for Durlan.

Something dark moved at the edge of my mind. I jerked my head in the direction, the woods beyond the town, and squinted my eyes.

"Something's out there," I said and stood, brushing my hands off.

Myrin and Daniel stood with me, their eyes focused in the same direction.

"That's a fae creature," Myrin whispered. "I can't tell what type, but that dark aura is unmistakable."

"We don't usually have something that evil here," Daniel whispered. "Did you bring it over on the ship on accident?"

I looked up at Myrin who shook his head. "We searched the ship well before leaving the port to make sure no Unseelie tried to stow away."

Birds flew up into the sky and away from the front middle of the forest where I sensed the creature. Then, the trees fell to the side as it shoved them aside to step out.

Ten feet tall, mud covered skin, and a red cap upon its head, the creature chittered loudly, a sound that made my skin crawl.

"A redcap," I gasped. It had been over a hundred years since a redcap had been seen in Minloa. How had one made it here?

"Get the others," Daniel yelled to Myrin as he shifted into his bear form and charged the redcap.

The humans near us screamed and scrambled to seek shelter in one of the buildings.

"Don't fight it," Myrin ordered me. "Get the weak humans to shelter and stand guard, but do not go out there and fight it."

I glared at him, but nodded.

He gave me a final, hard look, and then ran in the opposite direction to go get the others.

A pregnant mother with two toddlers hobbled towards a building, but she moved slowly. I gathered up her toddlers and urged her on faster. "Stay inside," I ordered them.

She nodded and the trio huddled together inside the building with several other humans.

Durlan stepped out of the building. "What's going on?"

"Redcap," I said. "Finish healing the humans. The others are coming to help."

His eyes widened. "A redcap? They have redcaps here?"

I shrugged. "Apparently."

Daniel made it to the redcap, and I froze as I watched the redcap swing his giant club at him. The bear dodged the club and bit the redcap's leg, tearing into the muscle and causing blood to spray before he leapt away, back towards the forest.

He was trying to lead the redcap back into the forest and away from the humans.

Some human men had come out with swords and spears, including some of the king's guards.

"Go back inside," I ordered them. "We'll handle this."

"What is that thing?" one of the guards asked.

"A redcap. It thrives on murdering things," I said. "Stay with your women and children. If we fail, you're their last line of defense."

"Will you fail?" a wiry man with wide eyes asked.

I smiled and turned to watch as the rest of my consorts ran into town. "No, they will not fail."

Venali's magenta eyes were focused on the redcap, the smile on his face evidence of his excitement for a fight.

Ryul stopped by me. "I'll stay with you, my queen."

I nodded. "Okay."

Venali stopped a dozen or so feet away from the redcap and roared. The sound was unmistakably a challenge.

The redcap turned, ignoring Daniel, and roared back.

Venali laughed and ran forward.

"Why isn't his sword drawn?" a human asked beside me.

"Because he doesn't want the battle to end too quickly," Ryul said. "He loves fighting."

"You're insane," the wiry man said.

I chuckled. "They are a bit unhinged."

Venali leapt up and punched the redcap in the jaw, the sound as loud as a thunderclap, and the redcap dropped to one knee.

"Get inside," Ryul ordered the humans.

"Check on Durlan," I said to Ryul. "Make sure he's not using too much magic."

He looked at me.

"I'm staying right here. Promise," I said.

He scowled, but jogged into the building where Durlan was.

Kydrus and Myrin stood off to the side, arms folded, and watched Venali and Daniel fighting the redcap.

Obviously, they didn't think their brothers needed help.

That quickly changed when five more redcaps ran out of the forest and roared their challenge.

CHAPTER 33
ELARA

My legs tensed, ready to help, but Ryul ran out of the building and pointed at me. "Stay."

I folded my arms across my chest and held my spot. "Fine."

He nodded and ran to help the others, his sword drawn.

Venali dodged one of the redcap's wild club swings, ran up the arm holding the club, and embedded a dagger into the redcap's eye.

The redcap bellowed and roared back, slapping at his face to try to hit Venali.

Venali bellowed with laughter and leapt off the redcap, landing lightly on his feet.

I wanted to tell at him to stop showing off, but he deserved to have some fun after the past few months I'd put him through. Plus, this was probably the first battle he had been in for over a hundred years at least.

One of the queen's guards poked her head out. "Is it safe for us to take the queen to her castle?"

"Ask Dakath to teleport you," I said.

Her eyes widened. "We could never ask a god—"

"Tell him it was my request," I said.

Durlan stepped out, the guard pointed at the castle, and he teleported them to it.

I sat on the porch and resumed eating my food while the guys fought with the redcaps.

While I'd been distracted, two of the redcaps had been killed, leaving four left for the guys to defeat.

The same feeling prickled along my neck, this time from the other side of the town.

A woman screamed in that direction.

I took off at a full sprint, my arms pumping as I raced to save the human.

I skidded around a building, bumped my shoulder into the building across from it, and slid around the other side.

Three recaps surrounded a woman and her daughter, both cowering on the ground and crying.

"Hey," I yelled at the redcaps.

They turned and snarled at me.

I reached for my sword, but hadn't brought it with me for the meeting. I sighed. "Hey, why don't you pick on someone a bit tastier," I said and strutted towards them like their evil aura didn't make my stomach turn.

The redcaps chortled.

"Your magic will be tastier than this human," the largest of the trio said.

I stopped, spread my arms to my sides, and said, "Come get some."

They roared and charged at me, clubs raised over their heads.

I drew on the sun's power and blasted the largest redcap through the middle of his chest with sun fire.

He fell to the ground, the hole sizzling and oozing.

His friends stopped, looking at their fallen comrade with wide eyes.

I examined my fingernails. "What's wrong? You boys scared of one little fae woman?"

They roared louder than before and descended upon me with clubs and claws swinging.

I leapt, dodged, ducked, and slid out of the way of their swings.

"I'm going to gnaw on your bones," one of the redcaps snarled.

Durlan teleported between the redcaps and me, his lips pulled back in a snarl, and said, "I don't think so." He punched the redcap who had threatened me in the jaw so hard that it came unhinged and dangled crookedly.

I opened my mouth to tell him I had everything under control, but watching my normally calm and logical mate beat the snot out of the redcaps was a huge turn on.

Plus, he looked like he needed to vent some rage.

He pummeled the two redcaps with his bare hands, broke their arms and legs, and then cracked their skulls open.

When the redcaps lay still, Durlan turned to me, eyes glowing and fangs bared, and said, "You are in so much trouble when we get home."

I smiled and asked, "Promise?"

His lips lowered, his rage receded, and he laughed while shaking his head. "Incorrigible."

I skipped over to him, stepping on top of the dead redcap

on his left to get up to his height and kissed his lips. "A lovable, incorrigible, handful that you couldn't live without."

He wrapped me up in his arms and kissed me back. "Yes."

"He killed them with his bare hands," the little girl yelled.

We both turned and I smiled. "Did you expect less from the god, Dakath?"

The mother and girl's eyes widened and before they could say anything, I took Durlan and led him back towards the other fight.

My other mates turned from where they stood over the bodies of the redcaps, their scowls almost identical.

"I'm alive," I called out and waved.

Only Daniel, still in bear form, and Ryul continued scowling while the others smiled.

I released Durlan's hand and skipped over to Venali, throwing my arms around his neck. "Did you have fun? You looked like you were having fun."

He swooped me up into his arms and kissed me deeply. "Lots of fun," he said when he pulled back.

"Where did they come from?" Ryul asked. He walked into the trees in the direction the first group had come from.

I hopped out of Venali's arms, hopped onto Daniel's furry bear back, and said, "Follow the broody one."

Daniel shook beneath me in what I assumed was a laugh as he loped after Ryul. The others followed.

I dug my hand into his fur and held on with my legs, like he was a horse.

"The humans are staring at us like we are insane," Amrynn whispered as he ran beside me and Daniel.

I shrugged. "We are to them." I looked around and realized Durlan wasn't with us.

"He went to finish healing," Myrin said.

I nodded and then gasped as we ran into a patch of forest that was black and looked burned.

Ryul grabbed Daniel and me, jerking us back out of the black area.

I clawed at my throat, the darkness blocking my airway.

"Shit," Kydrus hissed and dropped to his knees beside me, panting.

Ryul wrapped his hand around my throat, using his power to heal me.

Black tendrils of smoke floated from my mouth and dissipated in the air a moment later.

I fell into Ryul and gasped in air.

No. No. Not yet. He couldn't be here yet.

Myrin put his hands on either side of my face and forced me to meet his eyes. "He isn't here."

"It was a warning," I whispered hoarsely.

He nodded. "Yes."

Tears leaked down my face. "He's going to kill you again."

Myrin pulled me into his arms, and I sobbed against his shoulder.

I wanted to protect them. To keep my mates safe.

I wasn't strong enough yet. I needed to get stronger.

"Cleanse this area," Myrin snapped.

"Where are you going?" Ryul asked.

Myrin stood with me in his arms and walked towards the sound of roaring water. "To cleanse her. Daniel and Kydrus, come with us so you can be cleansed, too."

I let one hand drop and brushed my fingers through Daniel's fur. He licked my hand.

This had been a test. There was no doubt there would be more.

But why?

Why not just attack us now, when I was weak? What was he waiting for?

"We're all alive," Myrin whispered in my ear. "All of your consorts are alive. We need to be cleansed, but that won't take long. We are alive, Elara."

Yes, but for how long?

CHAPTER 34

DURLAN

"SHE WAS FIGHTING three redcaps by herself," I said to Kydrus. "She wasn't even in her goddess form."

Kydrus sighed and pinched the bridge of his nose. "I'd say I'm surprised, but I'm not."

I bent over the human before me and resumed healing him. All of these humans had a strange disease that, left untreated, would kill them. "I almost lost it, Kydrus. I haven't been so furious in a century. The one said he was going to suck on her bones and my vision tinted red. I can't remember the last time that's happened."

He patted my shoulder. "It happens to us all. Especially, when our lovely little goddess is involved."

"You know what her reaction was?" I asked, growling.

"What?" Kydrus asked, leaning his shoulder against the wall. He could have helped me heal these people, but they thought I was a god, so we were keeping up the ruse for now. Plus, I had plenty of power to heal them.

"She got turned on," I said and sighed.

He threw his head back and laughed.

"The woman will be the death of me," I grumbled.

"Can you blame her?" Venali asked as he stepped into the room.

I had no idea how long he'd been standing just outside, but long enough to hear my previous statement.

"What is that supposed to mean?" I asked.

"You're usually so reserved and logical. This was most likely the first time she's seen you go all protective mate mode," Venali said. He leaned against the wall beside Kydrus, giving him a pat on the shoulder.

"He's right," Kydrus said. "The only thing she's seen from you is calm and collected Durlan."

"I'm not always logical," I mumbled.

"More than most of us," Venali said.

"Says the man who laughed as a redcap tried to crush him," I said and shook my head.

"She really faced off against three redcaps by herself?" Venali asked.

I nodded. "There was a human woman and her child in danger. You know she can't ever leave the innocent in danger."

"You should have called me over," Venali said.

I grumbled, but made no coherent words.

"What he meant to say is that he let his anger get the better of him, so he didn't want to share his kills," Kydrus said, smirking smugly.

I flipped him off, finished healing the human, and stood.

The human sat up and asked, "Am I really healed?"

I nodded. "You should rest another hour or so and then you'll be fine."

"I won't die?" he asked.

I shook my head. "Not from this disease."

He got to his knees and bowed. "Thank you, Dakath. Thank you."

Dakath. It had been so long since I'd heard that name. I preferred Durlan now, but hearing it had brought back memories I had long forgotten and hadn't come back when the other memories did.

Most notably, the night before we'd died. That night, I'd been with Amara, trying to persuade her to go into hiding. She wouldn't have it. She'd wanted to fight alongside us and nothing I said would sway her.

"The past is in the past," Kydrus whispered. "Leave it there."

I stood and wiped my hands on my pants. "Let's go find Elara. I don't like leaving her with less than four of us at any given moment."

"Especially, since he made his first move," Venali said and snarled.

Yes. He was already moving against her, which made me uneasy. Everything about this attack made me uneasy.

It had been too simple.

There had been too few enemies.

It had obviously been a test, but a test of what?

I hated the unknown. I hated things that had no obvious reasoning, even flawed reasoning was better than none.

What would he do next? And how could I protect Elara from it?

CHAPTER 35

RYUL

CLEANSING the infected forest had been easy enough, but the lingering fear it left in me was the hardest to deal with.

Why set this up? Why teleport those redcaps to us?

Had he wanted to test Elara? To see if she would turn into Amara?

Or, was he trying to sully her before the humans? Had he hoped the humans would have been killed first and then she would have been blamed?

Amrynn walked at my side, silent and brooding like me.

"Do the humans make you uncomfortable?" I asked him.

He sighed. "Sadly, yes. I know they aren't the same ones. I know they don't have the same technology, but I still can't help feeling on edge around them."

"She feels the same," I said. "Myrin said he could sense her unease when we went before their monarchs."

He nodded. "Daniel said he could as well."

"What do you think about this trap?" I asked softly.

I wasn't certain where Elara was and I didn't want to discuss this with her nearby.

He looked up at the sky and exhaled audibly. "I'm afraid to voice my concerns. I hope, pray, that I'm wrong."

"Who do you pray to?" I asked with a chuckle. "We're the gods of this world."

He chuckled as well. "To whoever else might be out there. Someone who might listen and help us."

I scowled. "Do you think there are others?"

He shook his head. "There is only *him* and her. We're unique in that we were ascended because of her."

"Do you think he could have similar companions?" I asked.

Amrynn laughed. "I doubt it, but who am I to say? I would have sworn on everything in the universe that no human could have ever taken me captive and yet that is exactly what happened."

I felt for him, it was an awful feeling to be defenseless, helpless, or useless. Especially, when you had been undefeated for a millennium.

"It would have happened to any of us," I assured him and truly believed that.

"History is doomed to repeat itself, and I'm terrified of what that means for her," he said.

He wasn't terrified of what would happen to us, though. No, we were all willing to die again. So long as she lived.

"Things will be different this time," Amrynn said, his shoulders drawing back and determination setting his jaw.

I nodded. This time, I would not let my inexperience cause our downfall. I would bite my damn tongue and listen to Myrin.

He might be Unseelie, but he loved Elara and Amara. I

could see it every time he was near her or when he talked about her.

"Do you think the Seelie will accept the Unseelie?" I asked.

Amrynn smiled. "I don't think Elara will give them a choice."

"I thought Anderelle was bigger, but she's said there are only three continents. Is that right?" I asked.

Amrynn nodded. "She showed me a map of the planet before. Anderelle only has three continents, but several islands interspersed around those continents. The continents are large and take up a lot of the planet's space, but there is also a lot of ocean. I'd say the ocean makes up two thirds of the planet."

"Andrelle really has that much ocean?" I asked, eyes wide.

He wrapped an arm around my shoulders and squeezed. "Don't worry, I'll give you swimming lessons soon, so you won't have to fear the water anymore."

Had it been anyone else, I would have thought they were teasing me, but not Amrynn. He meant it.

"Thanks," I said softly.

"I've got your back, brother. Don't you worry your pretty head about it."

I scoffed. "You're the pretty one."

He laughed and drew away. "I am rather pretty, aren't I?"

"The prettiest there ever was," Elara said as she, Myrin, and Daniel walked out to the edge of the town where we were.

"I thought you were the prettiest there ever was?" I asked with a teasing smirk.

She blushed and my cock twitched in my pants. The fact that I could still make her blush turned me on and made me want to do very naughty things with her.

"Flatterer," she whispered.

"We should check on Durlan," I said.

She smiled. "You mean Dakath."

Amrynn smiled. "Yes, Dakath. It's been so long since I've heard that name."

She nodded. "Yes, but it helped. Now, I'm officially Empress."

"Empress of the Galaxy," I said.

Her eyes widened, and she hopped up to kiss my cheek. "Yes," she shouted. "Empress of the Galaxy. It's perfect."

Perfect was right in front of me.

I grabbed her, spun her around, and kissed her deeply. "You're perfect."

Her breath caught, and she clutched my arms. "If we weren't in public, I'd ask you to show me how perfect you think I am."

If I hadn't already had a hard on, I would now.

"Tease," I said with a smile.

She laughed, kissed my cheek, and extricated herself from my hold. "Sorry."

Oh, I didn't mind. She could tease me all she wanted. Every day for the rest of my life. As long as I could touch her, kiss her, and look at her like this, I was perfectly fine.

CHAPTER 36
ELARA

THE GUYS WERE in good spirits the next day, which I contributed not only to the fight, but also our marathon group session the previous night.

I lay in Amrynn's arms, naked, and content.

"Aren't you hungry yet?" he asked and kissed my temple.

"A little," I admitted. "But I'm so comfortable."

"You're meeting with the shapeshifters today, right?" Amrynn asked.

I rolled over and lay my head on his bare chest. "Yes."

"Then, you need to get up and eat. Daniel can't teleport, since he isn't fae, which means we have to walk there. He said it will take about half a day."

"Amrynn, stop being logical and just cuddle with me," I muttered.

He chuckled softly and pulled me as close as I could get. "Five more minutes."

I placed a kiss on his chest and smiled. It was moments like these that made all of the other bull crap worth it. To be able to lay in my mate's arms and just be together.

Our five minutes came and went, and with it another five minutes.

Then, Durlan peeked his head in and ordered us to get up for breakfast.

Reluctantly, I got dressed and went to the living room where the others already sat. Daniel didn't have a dining room, so we sat on the floor in the living room instead.

Myrin kissed my cheek and handed me a plate of food. "Sleep well?"

I nodded. "You?"

He smiled. "Yes."

Daniel patted the floor beside him, and I accepted the spot. As I sat, I leaned my shoulder against his. He was so much warmer than the rest of my mates.

"Anything we should know before meeting the shapeshifters?" I asked.

"They like fighting and are probably going to challenge at least one of them to a hand to hand fight," Daniel said. He looked around at the guys. "Probably Ryul."

"Why me?" Ryul asked.

Daniel smirked. "Because it is obvious that you're the youngest. And, you give off a vibe that just begs someone to punch you."

I choked on my food, and Myrin patted my back.

"Just be prepared for anything and don't kill anyone," Daniel said. "I'll do most of the talking, but they're going to want to ask you questions. Shapeshifters are inquisitive by nature."

"I want to speak to your historians, if there are such a thing," I said.

Daniel nodded. "The elders are the oldest and wisest of

us and know all about our history. I'm sure there are some books, too."

"Uh oh, don't tell her about the books. We'll never convince her to leave if she finds books," Venali said.

I stuck my tongue out at him.

"Let's pack some food for the trip and be on our way," Daniel said and stood.

I put on boots and lay on the couch as I waited.

How had my life gone from slave to goddess? It felt like an eternity ago that I was learning about being a princess and here I was trying to figure out how to unite the continents as their empress. Life was incredibly strange and unpredictable.

"You seem deep in thought," Durlan said. "What are you thinking about, beautiful?"

"How drastically my life changed," I said. "It's still unbelievable and yet...here I am."

"You've come a long way," Durlan said with a nod.

"Things are going to change even more in the next month," I whispered.

He set his hand on top of mine. "And we will be here, at your side, every step of the way."

I smiled and stood. "I love you."

He kissed my brow. "And I you."

"Ready?" Daniel asked.

I nodded. "Yep."

From the maps and research I had done, the continent was broken up into three sections, but ruled by two monarchies. The first section was where humans and shapeshifters coexisted together, ruled by the monarchs I'd met with the previous day. The second was the human only section, which those monarchs also ruled. Then, the shapeshifter section, which was ruled by a different monarch.

"How come you weren't monarch of the shapeshifters?" I asked Daniel as we walked out of his house.

"No matter how hard I tried, the majority of them wouldn't give up on their desire to live separate from the humans. They view the humans as beneath them, since they're weaker. I didn't want to rule people like that," Daniel said.

I tilted my head back to look up at him. "That's pretty moral of you."

He laughed. "Also, they have laws that the ruler must be mated. Since I wasn't going to mate with someone who wasn't you, that limited my chances of ruling."

I dropped my head and looked at the forest before us. If he hadn't had his memory, like the warlords, I could have come to find him mated to another. That thought hurt and infuriated me at the same time.

It also raised the question of why he and Myrin had their memories the entire time. They were the only non-Seelie members of my consorts. Did that have something to do with it?

Daniel draped an arm around my shoulders and tucked me against him as we walked. I rested my head against his side and drew in his scent. It was so much muskier than the others.

"What's your plan?" Durlan asked me.

"Talk to the shapeshifters," I said.

He sighed loudly.

"You should know by now that she prefers to figure things out as she goes," Venali said. "She'll get there and what needs to be done will just come to her. She doesn't work well with solid plans."

I turned and smiled at Venali over my shoulder. "Exactly."

Venali winked at me.

"Couldn't you form at least a broad plan?" Durlan asked.

"Talk to the shapeshifters. Convince them to name me Empress. Don't kill anyone," I said.

"Well, that is as broad as you could get, but definitely lays out your plan," Durlan said.

"Beautiful? When are you going to use your powers again? You need to practice," Kydrus said.

I tensed and pulled away from Daniel. I hadn't admitted it to any of the guys, but I was scared to use my powers again. *He* would sense me and likely set a trap or test for us again. I didn't want to use them unless necessary to limit our exposure to him.

"I'll practice more later," I said and picked up my speed.

Kydrus kept pace with me, his long legs easily matching my shorter ones. "We're going to be here to protect you, Elara. And, it might be good to have Amara speak to him."

"What?" Ryul, Myrin, and Daniel asked at the same time.

"If we could figure out a weakness that could help us defeat him, it might mean the difference between winning and losing," Kydrus said.

"He has a point," Durlan said. "Not that I want *him* to be anywhere near Amara or Elara, but if we could find a weakness it would help ensure our victory."

"Or, he could kill her before she's ready to face him," Ryul said.

"You're always so negative," Kydrus said to Ryul.

"No, I'm just practical. She isn't ready to face him," Ryul snapped.

"We have no idea how he will react to her. Plus, she can't hold her form for long. He might find her current state of existence upsetting and attack," Myrin said.

"Or, he might try to steal her," Venali said.

"Or, kill us," Daniel said.

They exploded into a yelling match and started getting into each other's faces.

"That's enough," I said.

No one listened.

I snapped my fingers and all of them froze. Eyes wide, I looked at my fingers and then at the guys.

Holy stars! I hadn't known I could do that.

Raising my head, I looked at them. "We will not discuss this anymore today. Do you understand? We have a lot of decisions to make and not very much time to make them. I don't want us fighting over something we have no clear answer for. No more fighting. Okay?"

They couldn't move, so I didn't wait for their responses.

I spun on my heel, marched away a dozen or so feet, and then snapped my fingers.

There were several groans, which told me they were moving again.

I smiled and swung my arms as I walked. I could freeze my consorts. That was so convenient. I could use this for so many things and in so many circumstances.

"Sorry," Kydrus said.

The others chorused his apology.

"You are forgiven," I said, trying to hide how chipper I felt.

"You're so proud of yourself for using that power," Myrin said with a chuckle. "I bet you didn't know you could do that."

"Nope, but I know how to now," I said in a sing-song voice.

"We're in so much trouble," Venali whispered.

I hummed a happy tune as I skipped through the forest, the guys chuckling behind me, and our argument, thankfully over. I had no doubt it was not forgotten, but hopefully it would not be brought up anytime soon.

CHAPTER 37

AMRYNN

ELARA WAS scared and that worried me.

She wasn't as fearless as Amara had been, which was a good thing, considering she didn't have all of her powers. Yet, she still found ways to drive us crazy by acting careless.

I wasn't sure how to react when Durlan told us about finding her fighting the redcaps. It was fitting to her character, but we were nearby and all she had to do was call. I would have teleported to her and protected her and the humans she wanted to help.

Watching her skip through the forest with a smug smile on her face helped lessen my worry. I loved seeing her smile.

Kydrus glanced at me, and we shared a grin. The frightened girl we had met was gone, transformed into a queen. I couldn't wait to see her change in the next few months, too.

"What's it feel like to shift?" Elara asked.

We all looked at Daniel, our curiosity probably as bad as Elara's.

Daniel hummed a moment before answering. "It's like a

good stretch. One second I'm this size and then I'm in my bear form."

"So, it doesn't hurt?" she asked.

Daniel shook his head.

"Do you feel stronger in bear form?" she asked.

"In a sense. As a bear, if I hug you, I can crush your body. Or, I could bite you with my much stronger teeth as a bear. In this form I don't have the thick canines that my bear form does."

I smiled at him, showing him my pointed teeth.

"Your teeth are weak," Daniel teased. "I could probably snap off that little fang with my human hand."

"You could try," I said, smiling broader.

Elara rolled her eyes.

Daniel laughed.

"Did you not know there were humans on this planet before you came to my town?" Daniel asked.

Elara's face closed down. "I did not. I can sense sentient beings and animals, but not what race. I assumed everyone on the planet was fey and thought humans were only in the solar system that I took."

"Took?" Daniel asked, his face screwing up. "What do you mean took?"

Had we forgotten to tell him about that part? We must have.

"Durlan?" Elara asked.

Durlan pulled his bag off, rummaged around in it, and then pulled out her crown.

All of our eyes were drawn to the sun and planets swirling within the crystals on her crown.

Fury filled me as I thought back to the humans of that

system and the way they had treated us. To Elara having her blood stolen while they kept her sedated.

"Amrynn?" Daniel whispered.

I looked away from the crown and realized everyone was staring at me.

Then, I realized that my lip was pulled up in a snarl. I lowered my lip and turned away.

Kydrus came to my side, a silent offer of support.

"So, these are their planets and their sun?" Daniel asked as he held the crown.

I kept my eyes away from it.

Had it been up to me, Elara would have crushed their planets in her fist and we would have been done with them forever.

Using them as an energy source was cosmic justice, but I wanted them dead. Especially, Barry.

Maybe I could convince her to pull Barry out and I could beat him to a bloody pulp.

Kydrus set his hand on my shoulder. "Breathe, Amrynn."

I exhaled.

"Will you have an issue working with the humans and shapeshifters, who are basically human?" Daniel asked.

I wasn't sure if he was asking me or Elara, so I didn't answer.

"There won't be a problem. I know these aren't the same humans. The humans who hurt me are trapped on the planets in the crown that you're holding," Elara said.

"Amrynn?" Daniel asked.

"Same," I said.

CHAPTER 38
ELARA

Seeing Amrynn react so strongly to the crown shocked me. I knew he still hated the humans of that world for what they had done to us, but I hadn't expected him to snarl at the crown.

He had seemed indifferent to the humans here, but I would have to keep an eye on him. And, I would need to talk to him.

"Can a human be turned into a shapeshifter?" I asked Daniel.

He shook his head. "No, you can only be born a shapeshifter if one of your parents is either a shapeshifter or a carrier of the gene."

"Carrier?" I asked.

He nodded. "Sometimes, the shapeshifting gene skips a generation."

Interesting.

"Are there any shapeshifters who have wings?" I asked. I would love to have a pair of wings.

Daniel chuckled. "No. There are only predatory

mammal shapeshifters. Well, at least that we know of. I suppose there could be others on a different continent that I've not seen. Here, though, there are no shapeshifters with wings."

Pity.

"If someone hurts you..." I began, but stopped.

He pulled me against his side and kissed the top of my head. "I can handle any of the shapeshifters we're going to see. I've fought most of them already. If I do get in a fight, you must not intervene. Do you understand? They aren't allowed to kill me, and couldn't, so even if you're worried you must not intervene."

"I don't like this. If I'm challenged, though, you must abide by the same rule," I whispered. I feared the only way I would get them to join me was to defeat them.

"We'll keep her back," Venali said.

If someone tried to kill any of my mates, it would take every living being on this planet to keep me from protecting them.

"She's got that look on her face that means trouble," Kydrus said.

"Isn't that just her face?" Myrin asked.

I turned to give a snappy retort but found him smirking. He was teasing me.

"Yes, I am always causing trouble," I said. "It keeps you guys on your toes."

"That's definitely true," Ryul mumbled.

I stuck my tongue out at him, and he dashed forward, trying to catch my tongue with his fingers, but I sucked it back into my mouth before he could.

"Too slow," I said in a teasing tone.

He smiled.

I stepped away from Daniel and Ryul took my hand, linking our fingers together.

All of this traveling and strategizing made for little alone time with each of them. It was something I needed to fix. None of them had complained, but I knew they wanted to spend some time alone with me. I wanted some time alone with each of them as well.

Sadly, it wasn't in the cards just yet.

We only stopped to relieve ourselves. Food was eaten as we walked, even.

We entered incredibly dense woods and the hair on the nape of my neck stood up.

We were being watched.

Daniel's shoulders tensed. "You don't want to mess with my companions," he said, though he didn't turn to look at whoever it was he spoke to. He continued walking, so we followed him.

I smelled smoke, but kept the observation to myself.

Several minutes later, we entered a clearing with several log cabins. We were definitely in Plunce now. There were hundreds of people walking around in various states of dress, or undress as the case may be. The variety of people genuinely surprised me, but if they were all shapeshifters, then their ease at being together made sense. Like was drawn to like, and though they differed in other ways, the thing that tied them together was strong enough to overlook the rest. Or, so it seemed.

I saw a few children, but it was mostly adults.

All eyes turned to watch our party as we headed towards

the largest cabin, where the smoke I had smelled was coming from.

Daniel opened the door to the cabin and bowed his head to me as I entered.

Inside, the cabin was unfurnished. Only chandeliers and wall sconces were present, both furnished with candles. There were six people, two women and four men, standing together at the other end of the cabin, talking quietly to each other.

"Alpha and council members," Daniel said. "I bring to you today the Queen of the Seelie."

All six turned to face us, and I could instantly feel their hostility.

"You've changed, Daniel," one of the men said. I'd forgotten that once our mate bond was solidified, he had started looking like the others, whose power never seemed to disappear, whereas mine had to be used sparingly.

"Seelie Queen?" one of the women asked.

I smiled. "Yes. I am Elara. It's nice to meet you."

"She doesn't look strong," the other woman said.

I smirked. "Neither do you, but I'm sure we both know that looks can be deceiving."

She returned my smirk with one of her own and then smiled broadly. "I like her."

Relief surged through me, but it was short lived.

"Who are all these men?" one of the men asked. He had a scar across his left eye, eerily similar to Venali's.

"Her warlords," Durlan said and stepped forward. "We are her advisors and—"

"Lovers," the second woman said, though there was no judgment or malice in the statement.

I tilted my head to the side. "How did you know?"

"You're covered in their scents. More so than just from being around them," she said. "And, your scent is on each of them." She turned her head and looked at Daniel. "Even you."

Daniel smiled. "Yes, she is my mate."

The woman who liked me gaped at him. "Mate? You took a mate? And a non-shapeshifter at that?"

Daniel looked at me, and I could see the love in his eyes as clear as the moon on a cloudless night. "Yes."

"Why are you here?" one of the men asked. He had a scowl that seemed never to waver. At least, it hadn't since we'd walked in. He looked older than the others, and the air of aggression surrounding him made me worry he would choose anything he could as an excuse to fight us.

"I am unifying our world," I said and took a step forward. "I ask for you to join us, to accept your place as equals amongst us."

They all laughed.

"Equals? You think you're equal to us?" the old man asked as he laughed.

Well, he wasn't scowling anymore.

"Let's take this meeting outside," I said and spun on my heel.

I sensed the old man move, gave my men a glare to hold, and as he came up to me, wrapped my hand around his throat and stared straight into his eyes, which were glowing amber.

"If you wish to test me, council member, outside is preferred so that I can trounce you in front of all of your people," I said sweetly.

I released him, and he snarled.

"You did not protect your mate," the first woman said to Daniel.

Daniel was snarling as he stared at the old man. "She ordered me to stay back. Trust me, if he tries to attack her from behind again, like a fucking coward, I will tear his head off before he touches a strand of her glorious hair."

The old man paled a bit.

Interesting. He was scared of Daniel.

"Daniel," I said softly. "I will accept their challenges in public. You will only be allowed to participate if I agree. Do you understand?"

"Yes, Elara," he said.

I turned back around and walked out of the building.

While we had been inside, most of the people had gathered before the building. Had they been expecting us to come out to fight?

Most likely from what Daniel had said.

"Shapeshifters," I called loudly. "My name is Elara. I am Queen of the Seelie of Minloa. I come to you today to ask you to join us as equals. To unify all of our continents in forming an open means of trade and communication. Together, we can accomplish much. Apart, we only suffer. Your council member has challenged me. I will accept his challenge. When I win, should another wish to challenge me, they may. You may also challenge any of my mates. However, these challenges will be to submission. If any tries to kill me or my mates, you will be obliterated without mercy. Understood?"

Everyone's eyes widened, including my consorts. Oh, right. I probably should have warned them I was going to do this.

I turned and faced the old council member. "Well, while

I have all the time in the world, I know your kind don't live for very long. So, we should get this fight over with."

He snarled, stalked to stand in front of me, and then he exploded into a large grey wolf.

He was so beautiful, I almost reached out to stroke his fur.

"You are beautiful," I whispered, letting my awe show.

His wolf eyes widened, and then he snarled, remembering why he was here.

I took a fighting stance, smiled, and said, "Begin."

He launched himself at me, trying to tackle me to the ground.

I spun around him and punched him in the side just below the ribs.

He flew to the side, landing against the other council members.

Whoops. I hadn't meant to hit him so hard.

He hopped up and began circling me while snarling.

I watched him with a loose stance, yawned, and asked, "Are you going to attack today? Or are you only good at attacking unsuspecting victims from behind?"

Several people snickered at my insult.

The old wolf barked loudly and lunged, his mouth wide and claws extended.

He moved so slowly. Daniel was much faster than him. Was it because of his connection to me?

It seemed I really had been worried for no reason about him fighting any battles.

I smacked the wolf on the back of his head, being sure to rein in my strength, and he immediately fell to the ground, unconscious.

I turned. "Who's next?"

The female who had spoken second stepped forward. "I am alpha of this pack. I will accept your challenge."

I bowed. "I am honored."

She smiled and turned to Daniel. "You want to take her place?"

Daniel smiled at me. "Elara, now would be a good time to show them who you really are."

"You don't think I can defeat her as I am?" I asked.

"I have zero doubt you could, but I think it will make our day go much faster," he said.

"But I'm having fun," I complained and stuck my lip out in a pout.

"I'll make you a deal," the alpha said. "If you show me who you truly are, and can defeat me in under a minute, we will join you without question. If I defeat you, or you take longer than a minute, you accept your defeat and leave us to be as we are, separate from the rest of the races."

"That's not much of a challenge," I mumbled.

Her eyes narrowed. "You underestimate me."

I shook my head. "No, you just have no clue who I am."

"Fine, I'll up the ante. If you defeat the entire council in a four on one battle, then we will join you. Five minutes will be your time limit," she said.

I smiled and turned to her people. "Will you abide by her decision?"

"We obey the alpha," they all said in unison, which was *super* creepy.

I faced her. "I agree to your terms."

Durlan held out my crown and I set it on my head.

"You may not want to wear that," the other male council

member said. "It would be a pity if something so pretty was destroyed."

"Oh, it'll be fine," I said.

One of the other shapeshifters had dragged the old man off to the side, giving me plenty of room to move. Not that I needed it. For the trick up my sleeve, I only needed a moment and the shapeshifters would be bowing to me.

"Elara," Daniel called.

I turned to face him.

"Do not go easy on them. Full force without killing. Do you understand? You must make them understand how powerful you are," he said.

I blew him a kiss. "Yes, dear."

The remaining council members shifted, but instead of animal forms, they shifted into half-man and half-animal forms. It was a beautiful and terrifying meld at the same time.

There were two wolves and two leopards between them.

"So beautiful," I whispered in admiration.

"Show us and try your hardest to defeat us," the alpha said. "We will not hold back."

I raised my arms above my head, drew on the power of my sun as well as the one in my crown and released my hold.

My body glowed, I rose up until my toes floated above the ground, and I heard several shocked gasps behind me.

The council members' eyes widened.

"Who are you?" the alpha asked.

"I am Amara, Goddess of this Universe, but for now you may refer to my proxy as Empress of the Galaxy. Let me end this, my precious children, so that you may become united, as you should have been this entire time," I said.

They charged forward, claws poised to attack.

I had to give them credit, they were still attacking despite being faced with a goddess and that took some guts.

"Kneel," I ordered them, pulling on all of the power I had at my disposal as I hit them with my command.

They struggled a moment, trying to fight the order, but all four dropped to their knees and bowed their heads.

My feet landed on the ground and I stepped forward to set my hand upon the alpha's head. "You are amazing and beautiful. The world needs your kind and deserves to know of your existence."

At the edge of my mind, I felt *him*. He reared up, his presence growing stronger and closer.

I had to end this now, before he reached me.

"Submit?" I asked.

"We submit," they all said at once.

He flew towards me, his dark power like a hurricane as he approached.

I released my powers and was glad that I had my hand on the alpha's head, or I might have fallen.

The darkness vanished, but I could still feel his eyes on me. This was not good.

Someone roared behind me and I turned, eyes wide, as the old wolf charged at me with claws barred and eyes glowing with a strange blackish tint.

I didn't have the energy to dodge fast enough. He was going to cut my face.

Daniel stepped between us, shifting into the half-man and half-animal form, his head completely a bear's, and roared at the wolf.

The wolf continued forward, crazed, and foaming at the mouth.

Daniel swung his pawed hand, slammed into the wolf, and sent him flying to the side, into one of the cabins.

The wolf created a hole as he flew through the wall and into the cabin, and then another hole as he exited out the other side.

"He's possessed," I whispered to Daniel. "Don't kill him."

Daniel growled.

"Ryul," I called. "Excise him."

Ryul stalked over to the wolf, who lay motionless on the other side of the cabin. He put his hands on the man's head, whispered something, and then leapt back as the darkness streamed out of the man and coalesced into *his* form.

"Amara, my love, stop this needless hiding and come to me. I do not wish to kill you again," he said.

"I am Elara," I said. "Leave me and my mates alone."

His eyes darted to my consorts.

"These men always get into our way. If I allow you to keep them for your amusement, will you come to me? Join me as you should?" he asked.

"You and I will never be joined," I said. "It is the natural order of the world for us to be separated. You know this. Stop trying to defy nature."

"Soon, my love, you will come to me. I hope it is before I break your spirit," he said and then the darkness disappeared.

Myrin wrapped an arm around my waist, without it I wouldn't have been standing.

"What was that?" the alpha asked.

"Evil," Daniel said. "He is the darkness to Amara's light." Daniel walked to me, his body back to human. He stood before me, his eyes fierce, but his touch gentle. "He will not win this time. I will not allow him to hurt you again."

"Is that what you're fighting?" the alpha asked.

I turned to face her. "It's why I'm trying to unite you all. Once all of my children are united, I can face him and not worry if I die."

"She's talking like Amara again," Ryul whispered loudly.

"We are the same, but separate, mostly," I mumbled.

"We lost and we will join you and this unified world you seek," the alpha said. "I do not wish to be ruled by that...evilness."

Yes, he had exuded evil and malice. I found it odd that she wouldn't want that, since they'd been so bloodthirsty.

"I think we should stay here tonight. Just in case he sends another trial," I said.

Durlan nodded. "I agree."

"Follow me," Daniel said. "I have a house nearby."

Myrin basically carried me as we walked behind Daniel while making it look like I was walking on my own.

"He's not going to stop," I whispered.

"We will win," Myrin whispered. "I'm sure of it."

"He will only stop once he has me," I said, tears filling my eyes. "Is this inevitable? Is this fate?"

Daniel held open a door to a log cabin that looked like every other cabin there. Inside was a giant bed, large enough to hold his bear form.

Myrin helped me inside, and then spun me to face him. "The only fate that exists is our fate of being together. Our love is fate. His terror is not."

I wished I could believe him. I did believe we were fated lovers, but I also knew *he* would never give up. He had said I could keep my consorts. Had he been honest? Would it be better to accept his proposal?

Myrin set me on the bed, and I immediately rolled onto my side and closed my eyes.

I needed a plan. I needed a plan that ended with my consorts alive and well. My life did not matter.

They had to survive.

CHAPTER 39

RYUL

His EVIL AURA had grown since the last time we'd fought him. Was he stronger? Was our fight impossible?

Elara had looked terrified when he'd spoken to her. Afterwards, she'd looked defeated.

That did not bode well for us. It made me incredibly nervous and worried.

If she didn't think we could survive, why should we? He was a god, while we were technically lesser gods, or half-gods.

As it was, Elara couldn't become Amara for more than a single magic use. He was already testing her and had come to see her in person. Would he increase these attacks and try to kill her while she was weak? Would she have time to learn to harness her powers more?

All of these unanswered questions, and that defeated expression on her face, made me antsy and ready to kill someone. But there was no one to kill.

"Breathe," Venali whispered in my ear.

I exhaled and loosened my hands which had clenched into fists in my lap.

"She's scared, but that's to be expected when she sees him for the first time. This will help her strategize for defeating him," Venali said.

"How can you be so sure? She looked utterly defeated," I whispered.

Venali looked over at Elara, sleeping peacefully on Daniel's bed. "Because I know her and I know that seemingly impossible tasks motivate her to overcome them."

"Does it not bother anyone else that people are agreeing so quickly to her becoming Empress?" I asked. "People who are supposed to be against mixing with other races just rolled over and joined."

Daniel turned to face me, his arms folded across his chest. He'd almost killed that wolf when he'd charged at Elara's back. It made me respect him a little bit more. "They faced a goddess and then met the dark god. They aren't stupid. They may be prideful, but they also want to continue living and know picking her side is the right decision."

"What if it's not?" I asked softly.

Daniel's eyes glowed as he glared at me. "I didn't realize you were such a coward now, Ryul."

I returned his glare. "I'm not a coward. I'm being practical. What if we lose again?"

"Then we all die," Myrin said, his eyes locked on Elara as they had been since she'd faced off against the dark god. "And this time, we won't come back."

"How do you know?" Durlan asked.

He'd been rather quiet this whole time, actually, all of them had been.

"I can't explain it," Myrin said. "I can just feel it. If we die this time, there will be no coming back."

"I don't think she plans on living past the battle," Kydrus said softly. "I think Amara plans to die and separate herself from Elara."

I'd gotten that sense as well.

Myrin's face fell. "Knowing her, that's extremely likely."

"What then?" I asked. "We go back to being the Queen of the Seelie's consorts?"

Venali turned to look at me, his eyes wide. "You have a problem with that? You didn't seem to have a problem being in that position before."

"That was before my memories were fully returned and I understood she was Amara, not Elara," I said.

"She's both," Amrynn snapped. "She is equally Amara and Elara. If we lose Amara, I'll be devastated, but will continue my life with Elara."

"I'm not saying I won't," I snapped back.

"I think everyone needs to take a breath," Durlan said and stood. "We don't know anything yet. *He* is likely to send one of his dark creations after her today or tomorrow. We need to be prepared. Bickering over what might happen won't solve anything."

"He's right," Venali said. "Let's set up rotations so we can properly protect her and the shapeshifters."

"I'll go out and do a perimeter check first," Daniel said and turned towards the door.

"We go as pairs," Durlan said.

"I'll go with him," Venali said and stood. "I need to stretch my legs."

Daniel nodded at Venali and the two left.

I sighed and leaned back against the couch with my eyes closed. They weren't taking my worries the right way. I wasn't going to leave Elara or Amara. That didn't mean I had to be okay with her plan. That didn't mean I couldn't be upset.

I had to think of the worst possible outcomes so I could prepare for them. That was how I worked. Talking about the "what-ifs" was my perimeter check.

"It'll work out," Kydrus said. "I do think we should look at every possible outcome, like the ones Ryul was discussing. It will help us develop plans ahead of time."

Durlan sighed. "You're right. I'm sorry, Ryul. I've not been myself since that redcap fight."

"Alright," Myrin said with a sigh. "Let's talk it all out. Hit me with your worst case scenarios, Ryul."

I sat up, eyes wide and looked at each of them. "Really?"

Myrin pinched the bridge of his nose. "Yeah. We're all on edge. I shouldn't take your strengths and the way you view things for granted. I'm sorry."

I never thought I'd ever hear Myrin apologize to me.

"Alright," I said and leaned forward. "Find some paper."

CHAPTER 40
ELARA

I stood before a mirror, looking at Amara instead of my own reflection.

"They must be protected this time," she said.

I didn't need to ask who she meant. "Yes," I answered.

"They won't like it," she whispered. "My plan."

"What plan?" I asked. Although we were the same, there were still thoughts and memories she had that I could not access.

"We will fight *him* first. Or try. If we fail, I will give myself to him. Not in your body, though. I will separate us. You will take our consorts and you will continue living Elara's life. You will rule over Anderelle as Empress."

I blinked. "You can do that?"

She chuckled. "I am a goddess, remember?"

"Why does *he* want you?"

She looked through me, likely viewing memories. "When we came into existence, there were more of us. Light and dark, water and fire, earth and wind. We were the gods of this universe. Together we represented balance. Fire and dark craved to possess everything. It is in their nature. We fought a long battle that nearly destroyed the universe. Dark absorbed fire and earth. Water and wind asked me to absorb them before they died, to help strengthen me. It wasn't enough. His desire to rule supreme and possess more power overruled everything else. I didn't know at the time, but the other elements had created the boys for me. They created my consorts. He had captured me and was going to force me to merge with him, when they came. They rescued me and our bond made it so that *he* could never absorb me. It infuriated him. He killed them for their insolence, as he called it. My loves, my consorts lay dead or dying on the battlefield and I had to do something. So, I took our souls and sent them through the stars, hidden from *his* sight. Then, when the time was right, our souls merged with newborns. My soul took a little longer to find you, but that is because you were the only one fit for me."

"Why me?" I asked.

"You harness the power of the stars. You were ideal."

"What about my mother?" I asked.

She shook her head. "Too meek. Her soul was not strong enough for the merger. Yours shone like a beacon in the night."

"Can we kill him?"

Amara's eyes pinched and she dropped her gaze. "I'm not certain. I do not think it wise to destroy him."

"So, we need to contain him?" I asked.

Her head whipped up, eyes wide. "What?"

"We need to find a way to contain him. So that we keep balance, but he cannot hurt us?"

She smiled wide and screeched like a young girl. "Yes. I

knew you were the perfect soul for me. Yes, we must figure out how to contain him. That will keep the balance but also keep us and our consorts safe."

"If we do that, what will you do? They love you. You are their mate. If you separate from me, they may go with you?"

And leave me behind.

Her gaze softened. "They love us, Elara. If we can contain him, I will figure out a plan for us and our consorts."

"Wait, does that mean their souls can be separated from their bodies?" I asked.

She shook her head. "I'm not sure why, but their souls fully merged with their host body. I could not separate them and give you your warlords while I keep my consorts."

Well, there went that idea.

"I will find a way that makes us all happy and try to figure out how to contain *him*. We must not merge more than is necessary to prepare your body for our attack. Twice a week. Do you understand? Any more than that and *he* will attack us. He may still, but I think that should keep him away," she whispered.

If only we had the technology that Barry and his planet had. I was certain they could figure out a way to contain the god. Or, would be better equipped anyway.

"That is a possibility," Amara whispered. "You would have to free their solar system to do so and run the risk of them capturing us again."

I scowled at her. "I didn't say anything out loud."

She laughed. "We are one. Don't forget that. Consider all of your options. I'd like to avoid freeing Barry. There must be a container on this planet. I had one, but it was lost. I will search for it. In the meantime, consult our consorts. We must figure this out, Elara. I won't lose them again. I will sacrifice myself long before I let them die."

I nodded. "That much we are in agreement on." I thought a moment. "Weren't there seven gods in the beginning?" I asked. I thought I'd read that somewhere.

She nodded. "Yes, I told you all of them."

I shook my head. "You only named six."

She counted on her fingers and her eyes widened. "I'm missing one. I can't remember. Who is it? Why can't I remember who the seventh is?" Her brows furrowed and she glared over my head. "Go to the men, they're probably worried because you're sleeping so much. I'll do some more research."

"I'll ask if they remember all the gods, too, but will keep from telling them you forgot one," I said.

"Okay," she said. "We will figure this out, Elara. It will work out for all of us."

CHAPTER 41

DANIEL

"You sure you don't want to go opposite me and meet in the middle?" I asked Venali.

He smiled. "Trying to get rid of me?"

"You want to talk to me, I take it," I said.

"Your powers started to show when you protected her from the possessed shifter," he said.

I sighed and dropped my head. "I overreacted. I sensed his bloodlust and the darkness when he neared."

"I wouldn't call that overreacting," he said.

"I threw him through a house," I reminded him.

He smiled wide. "That was very entertaining. It also made me really want to spar with you."

"That can be arranged," I said.

"You've been on edge," he said. "I thought you might need someone to talk to."

"I wouldn't say I want to talk," I muttered.

"You may not want to, but you should," he said.

"Aren't you supposed to be our brute?" I asked, snarling.

He beamed.

We continued walking, and after several minutes of his silent presence, I sighed and gave in.

"She's hiding something. I know you fae can't outright lie, but you can withhold information. She's withholding a lot. What I'm most worried about are the hints that Amara keeps dropping."

"What hints?" Venali asked.

"That she and Elara will separate at some point," I said.

He nodded. "I've been wondering about those as well."

"We cannot separate from these bodies. So, we would either be leaving Elara alone, or Amara. The thought of doing either is too much to bear. I don't know Elara that well, I know she is only the bearer of Amara's soul, yet just the brief time I've spent with her, having her by my side, I cannot imagine life without her. I'm sure it is even stronger for you guys," I said and glanced at him.

His eyes were pinched, and he nodded. "I love her—Elara. I also love Amara. I cannot imagine being without them at all. Yet, if she does separate, I would either have to choose, or they would choose for us, which makes my chest hurt, and pain unlike any I've known before course through me. I thought it would be easy to choose between them once I realized who she was and that she only had Amara within her, but I cannot. Elara is amazing and beautiful, and I love everything about her. I would not want to live away from her. Plus, I would not want to abandon her or leave her alone to be queen without us at her side. She would be devastated if we left her."

"So, somehow, we have to convince Amara to either fully merge with Elara, or at least stay within her," I said. "The question is, how?"

Venali nodded. "That is the question, but I have no answer."

Neither did I.

We finished our patrol and found nothing. I didn't think he would send us a test today. If my suspicions about him were right, he would send it tomorrow or the next day. He would try to let us fall into a false sense of safety, and then send monsters after us. Would it be more redcaps? Or something worse? I only knew about the fey monsters from my memories of our other lifetime. These people on Emortalia had never seen the evil fey creatures. I feared they were about to.

Just outside of the house, we could hear Elara arguing with someone, it sounded like Ryul.

"Does he always argue with her?" I asked Venali softly.

"He's trying to do what is right, but he never seems to go about it the correct way. He was like that with Amara, too. He has one goal, protect her. When she has plans that put her in danger, he doesn't want to hear it and wants to tell her how stupid she is being. Elara, much like Amara, does not answer well to that type of aggression. She digs her heels in and bares her teeth instead of backing down," he said. "He's better, but he is still learning how to convey his feelings to her. Some of us were born better at speaking to women. Also, while we were warlords, without our memories, we had over a thousand years of practice speaking to people and working out problems. He was in a castle, alone, waiting for her to return."

"So, he's not socialized properly," I said. Like a shapeshifter when we introduced them to humans, they had to be introduced slowly and learn how to react and interact with the humans.

Venali laughed softly. "Yes, I suppose you could word it like that."

"He loves her. I can see that. Maybe I'll try to give him some tips," I said. Not that I was an expert, but I had a lot of experience talking with volatile people and keeping them from exploding.

"Good luck," Venali said and pushed open the door.

We entered, and Myrin looked at us expectantly.

"Clear," I said.

He nodded and turned back to watch Ryul and Elara. Ryul and Elara were the only ones standing, the others were lounging on couches in my living room, watching the argument.

"You're being ridiculous," Ryul said. "You always want to put yourself in danger."

"I'm trying to save us, you buffoon," she snapped. "Why can't you see that?"

I leaned my shoulder against the doorway and smiled. She was really worked up, her tiny fists were clenched at her sides, the tips of her pointed ears were pink, and her teeth were bared, showing off her sharp canines. She was gorgeous and I wanted to throw her over my shoulder and take her to the bedroom.

I took a single step to the side to adjust my pants which had gotten tighter as I reacted to her.

Ryul had said something, but I'd missed it.

She yelled and threw her hands up in the air. "Impossible."

Myrin looked over at me and smirked. He was enjoying the show as well.

"What is your plan?" Durlan asked.

Elara tensed and pivoted so she wasn't looking at any of us. "It's complicated."

No, she just didn't want to tell us, which meant it was dangerous.

"You're not sacrificing yourself," Kydrus said.

She spun around with a deathly glare. "I didn't say I was."

He smiled. "You didn't have to. Most of your plans involve you trying to sacrifice yourself."

"I'm not saying I'm going to sacrifice myself," she said. "I just need to find something and it is hidden in a rather dangerous place."

"Which is where you being put in danger comes in," I said.

She lifted her head and met my eyes. The fire that burned within her, the strength that such a small body held, made my erection grow stiffer.

"What is it?" I asked her. "Or where is it?"

"Zenlop," she said.

The air rushed out of my lungs, and I saw everyone else in the room tense.

Zenlop was not a place anyone went anymore. It had been taken over by ruthless humans who murdered anyone who got close to their land.

Myrin stood, his fists clenched and said, "No."

She looked up at him, towering over her, and said, "You can't tell me no. I am going to Zenlop. You're either coming or staying here and pouting."

Well, that was a new stance from her I hadn't seen before.

"No ships have been able to dock there," Durlan said. "They're all blown up before they make land. How do you expect to get there?"

"I didn't say I had all the answers," she grumbled and looked away from Myrin to stare at the floor. "I have to go there. I have to. Somehow. I'll swim if I have to."

Ryul paled.

Right, he couldn't swim. We would need to fix that soon.

"Are you sure you can't find the item you need here or on Minloa?" I asked.

She nodded. "Positive. Amara said so."

I narrowed my eyes. She hadn't referred to Amara as a separate being before. Was that a bad sign? Did it have to do with the hints at them separating?

"Maybe we need to talk to Amara then," Ryul said.

Elara shook her head. "She said we couldn't merge except for twice a week. She doesn't want to risk darkness coming after us when we're still unprepared."

Venali looked at me, his scowl a mirror of my own.

"Why don't you and Amara fully merge?" I asked.

She looked back at the ground. "We can't."

I walked to her, took her tiny hands in mine, and said, "If you two separate, there's a chance that we won't stay with you."

She jerked her hands away from me and shoved around me. "I'm aware of the possible consequences. Far more than you seven." She shoved open the front door and said, "I'm going for a walk. Don't try to talk to me."

The door slammed closed behind her, and it felt like my heart had cracked with it. She was preparing for losing us.

"Amara is going to sacrifice herself, isn't she?" I asked softly.

"Seems that way," Amrynn whispered.

"She wouldn't make us choose if she didn't sacrifice herself, would she?" Ryul asked, his eyes on the door Elara had walked through.

"It's possible," Myrin whispered through clenched teeth. "That damn goddess never thinks about herself. If she's sacrificing herself, then she'll leave us with Elara. But, judging by Elara's reaction to your statement, there's another option they're preparing for, which would leave Elara without us." He growled and black flames licked up his arms from his clenched fists.

"Don't burn my house down," I ordered him.

He met my eyes, a challenge in them for just a brief moment, and then he closed them and shook out his hands, the fire disappearing. "Sorry."

I set my hand on his shoulder. "This isn't easy on any of us."

"She'd really make us choose?" Ryul whispered, horror etched across his wide-eyed expression. He sat on the couch and dropped his head into his hands.

"Or, leave Elara alone," Kydrus whispered.

"I can't let that happen," Amrynn said. "I won't leave her alone."

"Calm down," Durlan said. "We're not choosing. We'll convince them to merge. We need to figure out how to get to Zenlop."

"You're going to take her?" Kydrus asked.

"She's going," Durlan said softly. "Just like she was going to see the Unseelie and come here. We have two choices: follow her or wait and pray she returns. I'm not waiting behind ever again. I'm not being separated from her for weeks or months like last time, never knowing if she was alive or not."

"You're talking about when she was taken on the spaceship, right?" I asked. I felt so out of the loop. They'd been with her months longer than me, which irked me more than I would ever admit.

Durlan nodded. "It was torture."

"It wasn't a picnic for me either," Amrynn mumbled. "Damned humans."

"You know I'm mostly human, right?" I asked with an arched brow.

He looked over at me. "You're a demigod, not a human. And, I know not all humans are bad. Just like not all Seelie are good."

"What are we going to do about her?" Ryul asked.

"First of all, we're not going to tell her she's being ridiculous," I said and folded my arms across my chest. "Talking to her like that won't get you anywhere."

"She *is* being ridiculous," he said and stood.

"Yes, but if you actually want her to consider your side of the argument you can't call her names or say things like that," I said.

"You all baby her," Ryul said.

"No, we just know how to talk like adults," I said.

He snarled at me, but stayed in place.

"He's right," Durlan said. "You suck at talking to her. I think we need to teach you how to properly talk to people."

"I know how to talk to people," Ryul said.

"It's not your fault you were isolated," I said. "But it is your fault that you won't learn and change your ways. She's dealing with a lot of heavy crap and you're not helping the situation."

Ryul plopped down onto the couch. "Yeah, you're right. I'm sorry."

All of us stared at him in disbelief.

He glared back. "I'm not stupid. I can learn and accept when I'm wrong."

Well, there might be hope for him after all.

CHAPTER 42

ELARA

They were too damn perceptive.

I walked through the forest around the house, not straying too far, just in case *he* decided to send a test while I was separated from the guys. Not that he could know that, but I wanted to play it safe.

Amara had said that the item to contain *him* was on Zenlop. It was in a museum, on display for everyone to see. The item would be able to hold him and seal him inside for eternity.

But Zenlop was inhabited by humans, millions of humans. And not humans like here on Emortalia. No, these humans were like Barry, minus the scientific advancements, at least from what I'd been able to find out from the humans on Emortalia. The ones on Zenlop were more likely to kill someone than greet them. Especially, if they had pointed ears and teeth.

I still couldn't believe there were humans on my planet. I could sense lifeforms, but not what type they were. Were the humans here from Barry's system? Or were they always here?

There had to be a way for me to get to Zenlop and get the item I needed. It was our only hope of saving the universe.

Daniel's statement had hit too close to home. It had felt like he'd punched me in the stomach, despite only holding my hands.

I didn't want to lose them. I loved them. I didn't want to be the Seelie Queen without my warlords at my side. Just thinking about it brought tears to my eyes.

But...I didn't want to separate Amara from her consorts. They loved her. They were created *for* her. How could I come between a goddess and her consorts? I couldn't. I didn't want to force them to choose between us either.

That only left a couple of options, two of which ended with either Amara or I dying. I didn't want to die. I had so much life ahead of me, but what could I really offer? I wanted to unite the planet, but what good would it do if Amara was dead and *he* won? Or, if Amara disappeared and we no longer had her to protect the universe?

No, I couldn't be selfish. If I needed to die, then that was what I would do, or I would give them up and separate myself from them. If things started to look like it would end up that way, I would need to distance myself from them to try to ease the pain. No matter what I did, it would hurt. Losing them would be like losing half of me.

Even the thought of losing Daniel, who I didn't know that well, hurt immensely.

"You're crying," Myrin whispered beside me.

I looked up, realizing I had stopped beside the house, next to the bedroom. He must have seen me through the window and opened it.

"It's nothing," I said and wiped my face. "Just a lot to deal with and I'm not sure how to handle it all."

"Can I come out with you?" he asked.

He had been Amara's first consort, and we had the strongest connection. I could not deny it, even when I tried to remind myself that it was truly Amara he was connected to.

I nodded.

He climbed out of the window and held out his hand.

I bit my lip, debating. Should I start distancing myself now?

"Please?" he whispered.

Immediately, I set my hand in his, and he linked our fingers together.

Warmth radiated up my arm and into my chest.

Yes, this was right. Distancing myself could wait until I was sure I needed to.

"Thank you," he said.

We started walking, and I leaned my shoulder into his, and then my head against his shoulder.

"You aren't alone, Elara. We are here. We want to help you, to share your burden. You don't have to keep secrets from us. I really wish you wouldn't keep secrets from us."

"You'll be angry," I whispered.

"Possibly, but I'd rather be angry than scared and unsure, which is what we are all feeling currently," he said.

Putting myself in their shoes, I could understand what he meant.

"I don't want to make you choose," I whispered. "If it comes down to that, I won't make you choose."

"We don't want to choose," he said and his hand squeezed mine. "We love you and Amara. I don't want to be away from either of you."

"There might be a way to save the universe, but it requires me getting an item from Zenlop. I don't know how we're going to get there. Or how I'm going to get the item, but I have to. We have to. I think it is our only option," I said.

"What is the item?" he asked.

"A pot," I said.

He looked down at me with an arched brow. "A pot?"

"It's a special pot. The humans there don't know that it is anything other than a very old pot. It was actually Amara's, but it had been stolen at some point and now it is in a museum there."

"Humans? Did you say humans are on Zenlop?" he asked, stopping and turning to face me.

I nodded.

"Amrynn is not going to like that at all," he whispered.

I sighed. "I know. He's still not over what happened with Barry." Not that I was either.

"If we get the pot, then what?" he asked, nudging me back to walk again.

"I don't want to say it out loud, in case *he* is listening," I whispered.

Myrin sighed. "That does make sense, but it infuriates me."

I laughed and hopped up to kiss his cheek. "I'm sorry."

He spun me sideways, his arms wrapping around me, and pushed my back against a tree. "Your life has value, Elara. Even if Amara separates from you, you are a person who deserves to live a long and happy life. I will do everything in my power to ensure you survive this and go on to live a happy life as Queen of Minloa."

I swallowed thickly. "Sometimes sacrifices are necessary."

He trailed his fingertips down my cheek. "Yes, but your life is not one of them. I will sacrifice myself to save you. I failed Amara, but I will not fail you."

"I'm just a Seelie girl. I may be of noble blood, but I'm nothing in the grand scheme of the universe. Just a speck that will disappear before long. Your life is worth more."

He shook his head. "That's where you're wrong, my love. You will change the world. I will not. I was created as a tool. To fight and protect." He smirked. "And for pleasure and companionship."

His companionship was definitely pleasurable.

"Now that you know I'm not Amara, that we are separate, shouldn't it feel wrong to be my mate?" I asked.

He kissed me lightly. "Does this feel wrong?"

I shook my head, my heart pounding in my chest.

"No. You are my mate just the same as I am Amara's consort. I will do this until I am forced to stop, or you tell me no." He pressed his body against mine, pinning me to the tree and kissed me deeply.

I moaned into the kiss, wrapped my arms around his back, and gripped his shirt. He was my rock, my ever present and steady mate. He grounded me in a way that I didn't really understand, but wasn't going to try too hard to.

He pulled back, unbuttoned my pants, while staring at me, waiting for me to stop him.

We were in the middle of the woods outside of Daniel's house in the shapeshifter town. At any point, someone could walk by and see us.

That made me want to do it even more.

I reached out and undid his pants, gripping him once free.

He groaned, and his eyes rolled up into the back of his head.

"This will be quick," he said in a way that sounded like an apology.

I turned around, and he wasted no time slipping inside of me. I gasped in pleasure and arched into him.

He gripped my hip with one hand and reached up to fondle one of my breasts with the other hand. "You're my mate, Elara. I won't give you up without a fight. I want to be doing this with you for centuries to come."

I leaned forward to give him better access, gripping the trunk of the tree.

He growled softly and slammed fast and hard into me.

I screamed as I orgasmed and almost immediately orgasmed again.

Our session was short, but we both found the release we needed, and for some reason, it felt like our bond was a little bit stronger.

After redressing, I leaned against him, hugging him tightly. "We can do this, right?"

"Go back to the house?" he asked.

I looked up at him with a frown. "You know what I mean."

"Let us work with you. Talk with us. We can do anything if we work together," he whispered.

I nodded and stepped around him.

We returned to the house and my mind was made up. I would go to Zenlop, I would get the container to seal the dark god inside, and I would spend every last second I could with these men, until they were taken from me.

Then, I would learn to live without them.

CONTINUE ELARA'S STORY

Continue Elara's story with Book Three of Their Fae Goddess Series, GODDESS OF THE UNIVERSE

ABOUT THE AUTHOR

Catherine Banks is a USA Today bestselling fantasy author who writes in several fantasy subgenres and has multiple pseudonyms. She began writing fiction at only four years old and finished her first full-length novel at the age of fifteen. She is married to her soulmate and best friend, Avery, who she has two amazing children with. After her full-time job, she reads books, plays video games, and watches anime shows and movies with her family to relax. Although she has lived in Northern California her entire life, she dreams of traveling around the world. Catherine is also C.E.O. of Turbo Kitten Industries™, a company with many hats including being a book publisher and Etsy store full of nerdy fun.

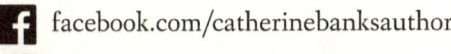 facebook.com/catherinebanksauthor

twitter.com/catherineebanks

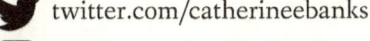 amazon.com/author/catherinebanks

bookbub.com/authors/catherine-banks

MORE FROM CATHERINE BANKS

YOUNG ADULT PARANORMAL & FANTASY ROMANCE SERIES

Artemis Lupine Series
Song of the Moon
Kiss of a Star
Healed by the Fire
Battles of the Night
Artemis Lupine, The Complete Series

Little Death Bringer Duology
Mercenary
Protector
Little Death Bringer, The Official Coloring Book

Pirate Princess Series
Pirate Princess
Princess Triumvirate

ADULT PARANORMAL & FANTASY ROMANCE SERIES

Zodiac Shifters Paranormal Romance Series

Centaur's Prize

Tiger Tears

Lion About

Ciara Steele Novella Series

True Faces

Barbaric Tendencies

ADULT REVERSE HAREM PARANORMAL & FANTASY ROMANCE SERIES

Her Royal Harem Series

Royally Entangled

Royally Exposed

Royally Elected

Royally Enraged

Her Royal Harem, The Complete Series

The Demon's Fair

Her Royal Harem, The Coloring Book

Wings of Vengeance Series

Of Dragons and Cruelty

Of Minotaurs and Sacrifice

Wings of Vengeance, The Complete Series

Their Fae Goddess Trilogy
Queen of the Stars
Empress of the Galaxy
Goddess of the Universe
Their Fae Goddess, Complete Trilogy

Bonds of Madness Series
Sealing the Deal

Her Super Harem Series
Lucky Strike

VELLA ADULT PARANORMAL REVERSE HAREM ROMANCE
Shark (Season One)
The Golden Alicorns (Season One)

MORE FROM CATHERINE BANKS

STANDALONE YOUNG ADULT PARANORMAL & FANTASY ROMANCE BOOKS

Monster Academy

Daughter of Lions

Lady Serra and the Draconian

Of Sky and Sea

The Last Werewolf

Sybil Deceived

An Outcast Among Wolves

STANDALONE YOUNG ADULT PARANORMAL & FANTASY REVERSE HAREM ROMANCE BOOKS

Moon Academy

Claws & Wings

STANDALONE ADULT PARANORMAL & FANTASY ROMANCE BOOKS

Dragon's Blood

Last Ama Princess

Transforming Rose

Alys of Asgard

Phoenix Possessed

Stone Heart

STANDALONE URBAN FANTASY BOOKS

The Pawn

CHILDREN'S BOOKS

Calvin's Alien Adventure

MORE FROM DAISY EMORY

The Boyfriend Deal

Their Purple Girl

ACCIDENTAL MOBSTER SERIES
Accidental Mobster
Unintentional Pirate
Suddenly Baroness
Unexpected Assassins*

LIPSTICK & LEATHER SERIES
Trinity
Alicia*

*Coming Soon